力得文化
Leader Culture

宜璞◎著

U0077353

職場英語
占♥術
為人見人愛的職場大贏家

要會的情境式英語 ➕ 一定要看的心理測驗
➖ 創造雙贏的局面

知己知彼百戰不殆
除了瞭解敵我，更要能超越敵我

職場五大情境：**辦公室、貿易、業務、行銷**加**感情**

要看的心理測驗：每個單元後皆有心理小測驗，藉由簡單選項，測出自我性格，

了解自我心理內在變化。也能與人分享，一窺對方**性格**及**心中想法**

要會的情境英語對話：擬真職場英語對話實境包含有職場常用詞彙、實用好句型，

活潑有趣的內容讓人覺得**好記、好看、好好笑**。熟悉詞彙用法及各式好句型，

靈活運用在職場上，將能不斷**超越自我**，讓同事、商業伙伴及上司**刮目相看**

還有心理常識補一補：對應情境的心理小眉角，讓你的職場關係**不「突槌」**

作者序

　　英文有分很多場合及時機，商業英文就是其中一種，職場上並非只有嚴肅，大家也是有血有肉有感情，也是會開玩笑的。學英文可以很有趣，只要你拿掉先入為主的觀念並帶著熱情去探索，不要怕去講，錯了就錯了，可以溝通就贏了。

　　本書分為28個單元，以模擬對話的方式切入每一主題，在每一主題中也有實用句子，並衍生出專業或生活化的「好好用句型」讓你在說的時候有更多種的選擇。對話偏向於職場生活化的感覺，讓你不失專業卻也同時生活化及真實。從對話中又延伸出每個對話主角心中的OS，再由筆者附上精選的心理測驗及補充相關的心理知識。本書結合商業英文與心理學，希望以不枯燥乏味的方式學習商業英文，也希望每個主題在讀者閱讀時是很有畫面的。

何宜璞

目次
Contents

目次
Contents

Part 1
辦公室篇

Part 1

Unit 1 社會新鮮人報到

 前情提要

Tom and Jerry are the newly-hired employees going to report for duty and make a self-introduction to their colleagues in the office today.

Tom 和 Jerry 是新聘的員工要去報到且今天要在辦公室裡對他們的同事做自我介紹。

 角色介紹

Terry- Manager of HR Department（人資部經理）

Tom- Newly hired employee 1（新聘員工 1）

Jerry- Newly hired employee 2（新聘員工 2）

David- Colleague of Tom and Jerry（Tom 和 Jerry 的同事）

 情境對話

Terry: Good morning everyone, please come and meet our new staff members, Tom and Jerry to join this big family.

大家早啊，請來認識我們的新成員，Tom 和 Jerry 來加入我們這個大家庭。

Tom: Thanks Terry. Hi everyone, my name is Tom or you can call me Tommy if you like. I have been in this industry for 8 years and I am grateful to be

謝謝 Terry。大家好，我的名字是 Tom 或者你們喜歡的話可以叫我 Tommy。我在這個行業

recommended to this company, I am sure there are still a lot of things here for me to learn, but I am a quick learner so I should be alright. I am outgoing and quite handsome as you may have already noticed. Anyway, it is really nice to be here with you guys.

已經有 8 年了,而我很感謝被推薦到這家公司,我確定在這裡還有很多我要學的東西,但我學得很快,所以應該沒事的。我外向,也蠻帥的你們可能已經注意到了。總之,在這裡跟你們一起真的很好。

Jerry: Morning everyone, I am Jerry, nice to meet you all.

大家早安,我是 Jerry,很高興認識大家。

Terry: Okay, Jerry is obviously very shy and Tom talks too much. Is there anything else you would like to ask Tom and Jerry?

好的,Jerry 顯然是很害羞,而 Tom 話很多。你們是否有任何其他想問 Tom 和 Jerry 的?

David: Hi I am David. I just have one question, and we have a welcoming party for all the newcomers tonight, would you like to come?

你好,我是 David,我只有一個問題,我們對所有新來的有個歡迎會,你們想來嗎?

Tom: Sure, why not?

當然,為什麼不要。

Jerry: I am not sure; I will let you know later.

我不確定,我等等再讓你知道。

Part 1

 前情提要

Jenny is in the office asking how David thinks and sees in two of his new colleagues-Tom and Jerry.

Jenny 在辦公室裡問 David 對於她的兩個新同事–Tom 和 Jerry 的看法。

 角色介紹

David- Colleague of Tom and Jerry（Tom 和 Jerry 的同事）

Jenny- Manager of Tom and Jerry's department（Tom 和 Jerry 部門的經理）

 情境對話

Jenny: Hey David, how do you think of Tom and Jerry? Have you got any chance to get to know them?

嘿 David，你覺得 Tom 和 Jerry 怎麼樣？你有任何了解他們的機會嗎？

David: Jerry does not really talks to people and even if he does, **you can barely get words out of him as he is not fond of speaking**, and Jerry never goes out for lunch, he brings one sandwich from 7-11 as his lunch every day, always a tuna sandwich.

Jerry 不太和人說話，而且就算他會，你也不太能讓他說多少話，因為他不愛講話，還有 Jerry 從不出去吃午餐，他每天從 7-11 帶一個三明治當午餐，總是一個鮪魚三明治。

Jenny: That is somewhat special, special in a weird way though, how about Tom then?

這是有點特殊的，但是是奇怪的那種特別，那麼 Tom 呢？

David: Tom is like the opposite of Jerry. **Tom is so easy to get along with,** and you are just so comfortable to be around him; **he is like the office clown that makes people laugh all the time**; however, he at the same time can be very professional at work when we need him to, he has a clear mind knowing what he is doing and get works done perfectly.

Tom 就像是相反的 Jerry，Tom 是很容易相處的而且你在他身邊就很舒服，他就像辦公事裡的開心果總是能讓人笑，然而他卻也能在我們需要他很專業時很專業，他思緒清晰，知道自己在做什麼，然後完美的做好工作。

Jenny: Well, I do not really pay much attention on Jerry, and I feel the same about Tom, but I have to admit I had a bad impression about Tom as I thought he is just an arrogant guy, but now I have learned that he is really something.

這個嘛，我沒有太注意到 Jerry，可是對於 Tom 的感覺是一樣的，但我必須承認我對 Tom 有不好的第一印象，因為我以為他只是個很自大的人，但我現在了解了他是真的有兩把刷子的。

Part 1

 辦公室心情隨筆

 Tom:

Okay, now I am in this new company, I am so going to be fine because I always make friends quickly, and people just like me for being me. I make people feel comfortable and easy to be around. Besides, I am not ugly. That should, give me some points in the beginning . Moreover, this job is the job I know I can handle and be good at. With my experience, I only need a little training and some time to be very good at things . It is nice that they are holding a welcoming party for us, so I can use that chance to make new friends, and I love parties.

好，現在我是這家公司的新人了，我一定會沒事的，因為我總是可以很快交到朋友，而且人們就是喜歡我。我讓人們在我身旁都很舒服也輕鬆。此外，我不醜，這樣應該可以在一開始先幫我加分。再來就是，我知道這份工作我能勝任，也可以做得很好，以我過去的經驗，我只需要一些訓練，和一些時間就可以做的非常好。他們要為我們辦一場歡迎派對真好，我可以藉那個機會去交新朋友，我愛派對。

Jerry is also new in this company, but he does not look experienced at all. Why is Jerry that shy? Maybe I can be a friend of him first since we are both new, and I should ask him to go to that party with me and get him to make some new friends as well. If he is not a party person, I will just go alone then. I cannot wait to go to that party and start over in here.

Jerry 在這家公司也是新人，但是他看起來一點都不像是有經驗的。為什麼 Jerry 那麼害羞？因為我們兩個都是新人，也許我可以先跟他成為朋友，然後我應該叫他和我一起去那個派對，然後讓他也交一些新朋友。如果他不是愛派對的人我就自己去就好了。我等不及要去那個派對，還有在這裡重新來過了。

Jerry:

This Tom is also a new guy like me, but he seems so easy and not nervous at all. He said quite a lot about himself, what should I say about myself? Maybe I will just simply say hi and let this be over soon.

這個 Tom 跟我一樣都是新人，但是他看起來好自在而且一點都不緊張。他說了好多介紹自己的話，我要說我自己什麼呢？也許我就簡單打個招呼讓這個趕快結束好了。

There is a welcoming party for us? Should I go? I do not really go to parties because I always feel embarrassed in parties, but the party is for all the new staffs, maybe I should go and see if I can meet someone as shy as me and we can be friends. Instead of going with Tom, I think I should probably go by myself because if I go with Tom, he will definitely drags all the attentions on him. However, missing this party might lose a chance to get to know other colleagues, and I am too new in this industry; I really need to work on my connections. Okay, I will go.

有個為了我們而辦的歡迎派對？我該去嗎？我不太參加派對的，因為我在派對裡總是覺得尷尬，但是派對是為了所有新職員而辦的，也許我應該去看看可不可以認識到和我一樣害羞的人當朋友。比起和 Tom 一起去，我覺得我應該自己去，因為如果跟他去，他會把所有注意力抓去他身上的。然而，錯過這場派對可能也會錯失認識其它同事的機會，我在這個產業裡太新了，我真的需要好好來建立一下我的人脈。好吧，我會去的。

辦公室篇

貿易篇

業務篇

行銷篇

感情篇

Part 1

★ **You can barely get words out of him as he is not fond of speaking**

你也不太能讓他說多少話因為他不愛講話。

He is not fond of speaking.

他不愛講話。

> Or you can say:
> - He does not like to talk things to death.
>   他不太愛講話。
> - He is so buttoned up.
>   他是很沉默寡言的。（ buttoned up 也有守口如瓶之意）

★ **Tom is so easy to get along with.**

Tom 是很容易相處的。

easy to get along with

容易相處的

> Or you can say:
> - easygoing / free and easy
>   好相處（皆形容人好相處，常用說法）
> - an easy person to be with
>   一個好相處的人

★ **He is like the office clown that makes people laugh all the time.**

他就像辦公事裡的開心果總是能讓人笑

He is like the clown.

他就像開心果。（ clown 原意為小丑，小丑帶給人歡笑故在此有開心果之意。）

- He is a real delight.
  他是開心果。
- He makes everything more fun.
  他讓一切變得更有趣。（即有開心果之意）

 **心理小測試**

社交活躍度

Q 假如你有強大的藝術才能讓你能流芳百世，如果讓你擁有可以展示在羅浮宮藝術殿堂裡擺放自畫像讓人景仰的機會，你的這幅自畫像你會希望是用什麼方式呈現的呢？

A：以油彩畫的方式呈現

B：在黑板上以粉彩畫的方式呈現

C：以水彩畫的方式呈現

D：以炭筆素描畫的方式呈現

辦公室篇

貿易篇

業務篇

行銷篇

感情篇

測 驗 結 果

A：你是個蠻沉迷於出席社交場合以及喜歡出風頭的人。你喜歡
參加超級奢華或者有噱頭的宴會或是派對，因為你天生就是
個萬人迷。你擅長在公眾場合下輕鬆的展現自己獨特的魅
力，輕而易舉就可以成為全場焦點。

B：你在社交場合中所扮演的角色是不可忽視的，對於那些愛口
若懸河的社交份子來說，你永遠是最好的聽眾。你的存在能
帶給大家滿足感和成就感。你很自然的表現出對朋友的關
心，讓大家在你身旁都覺得很溫暖。

C：你是個擅長製造小氣氛的人，你是個很適合辦些朋友聚會或
者小主題派對的人，和三五好友的溫馨下午茶聚會，是很適
合由你主辦和張羅的。

D：你是屬於喜歡以自我真實面目待人的人，對於外表和言辭也
不喜歡做過多的修飾，你待人誠懇，不偽裝和隱藏自己的想
法。但是你在別人眼中的評價卻很兩極，不是大好就是大
壞。你特立獨行的風格，想取悅所有人是蠻難的。

心理知識補一補

◈ 第一印象

　　第一印象（first impression）是長期交往的基礎，也是取信於人的出發點。因此，不論是在職場上或者跑業務的時候，能讓人留下好的第一印象是很重要的。

　　第一印象之中的月暈效應（Halo effect）是指在人際交往中，往往會將其某些特質擴大解釋，例如我們對於外型姣好的人會有較好的第一印象，也可能會認為其能力也不錯，就像我們看到的月亮大小，不是實際上月亮的大小，而是包含了月亮的光暈。當一個人留給他人的印象是「好」時，就容易把他的言行舉止用「好」的角度去解釋。反之，若一個人給人「不好」的印象時，那麼，一切不好的看法都會加諸在他身上。這種現象就是「月暈效應」，也就是俗話說的「以偏概全」，英文中稱為是"Stereotype"。

透過以下心理學的建議，建立良好的第一印象：

1. 放鬆臉頰與肢體
2. 增加視線交會
3. 製造意外的驚奇：公事之外談談自己的興趣，能創造意外感。
4. 在好氣氛下告別：能讓人期待下次再見面。

辦公室篇

貿易篇

業務篇

行銷篇

感情篇

Unit 2 空降老闆

 前情提要

There is an operation manager job opening in the AB Company, three employees are discussing about whom among them might take over this job.

AB 公司有一個營運經理的職缺，三個員工在討論他們之中誰會接手這個工作。

 角色介紹

John- Currently being the operation manager of AB Company but will be leaving soon. （目前是 AB 公司的營運經理，但很快會離開）
Haj- Employee 1 of AB Company（AB 公司的員工 1）
Warren- Employee 2 of AB Company （AB 公司的員工 2）
Louis- Employee 3 of AB Company （AB 公司的員工 3）

 情境對話

Louis: Have you guys heard about the news regarding John's resignation?

你們有沒有聽説關於 John 要辭職的消息？

Haj: Is that true? When will he leave? I have been working really hard for this firm; I hope I can get the chance to be promoted.

這是真的嗎？他什麼時候要離開？我在這個公司一直很辛苦工作，我希望我能得到這被晉升的機會。

Louis: He will be gone by Monday, but how about me? I often work until late and I got quite a few projects well done and well-organized.

他星期一就離開了，但是那我呢？我常常工作到很晚，而且我有不少計劃做得很好也策劃的相當完善。

Haj: That is right, but do not forget about Warren, John trusts him a lot and Warren is such a talent!

是沒錯，但別忘了 Warren，John 很相信他，而且 Warren 真的很厲害！

Warren: Hey, I overheard all of your conversations, but I do not think I am capable for being an operation manager.

嘿，我無意中聽到了你們所有的對話，但是我不認為我有能力可以當一個營運經理。

Louis: We will see about that, I might have less work experiences than you two, but all three of us have the opportunity to get this promotion.

到時候就會知道了，我工作經驗也許比你們兩個還要少，但我們三個人都有機會得到這次的升遷。

Warren: Maybe I should recommend Haj to the board, since I know you can do it better than me and you do things efficiently.

也許我應該向董事會舉薦 Haj，因為我知道你可以做得比我更好，而且你做事情有效率。

Haj: It is too late for the recommendation I think, they will post the announcement on Monday.

現在要推薦我想為時已晚了，他們禮拜一就會貼公告了。

Part 1

 前情提要

Josepha is the new operation manger of AB Company, recently graduated from a U.S. university without any actual work experiences.

Haj, Warren and Louis are going to find out about this arrangement from an announcement.

Josepha 是 AB 公司新的營運經理，最近剛從美國大學畢業，沒有任何實際工作經驗

Haj，Warren 和 Louis 將會從公告上得知這件事

 角色介紹

Josepha- The new operation manager of AB Company.

Haj- Employee 1 of AB Company（AB 公司的員工 1）

Warren- Employee 2 of AB Company（AB 公司的員工 2）

Louis- Employee 3 of AB Company（AB 公司的員工 3）

 情境對話

Louis: No way! Josepha Caswell? Have you seen that announcement? Our new operation manager! Who is this Josepha anyway!

不可能！Josepha Caswell？你有看到那公告了嗎？我們的新營運經理！到底這個 Josepha 是誰！

Haj: Yeah I know! **Also what is all that hoping to "shake things up" theory...** How can he just come out of nowhere to take over my job!

有，我已經看到了！還有那些所有什麼希望「改革」的理論……，他怎麼能就這樣不知從哪冒出來的來搶我的工作！

I heard he knows nothing about our products, and he just graduated from the U.S. Maybe there is something I did wrong.

我聽說他完全不了解我們的產品，然後他才剛從美國畢業而已。也許是我做錯了什麼。

Louis: I do not know, but we gotta tell Warren about this!

我不知道，但我們要告訴 Warren 這件事！

Warren: I am just right behind you guys! **Actually, I do not really mind having someone just parachuted into this position.**
He might have limited knowledge of our products, customers, and competitors, but we can assist him, there is a reason they picked him.

我就在你們後面！其實我真的不介意別人就這樣空降到這個位置上。

他也許對於我們的產品，顧客和競爭者的了解有限，但我們可以協助他，他們選他有他們的原因。

Haj: It is just hard for me to accept the facts that all our hard works do not count and I really wish I got this job, not him. This upsets me.

只是我真的很難接受我們所有的努力都不算數，而且我真的希望得到這工作的是我，不是他。這讓我心情不好

Louis: So true. I doubt he can be the leader in our field.

說的很對。我懷疑他能在這領域中帶領我們。

Warren: **Time will tell.**

時間會證明一切。

辦公室篇

貿易篇

業務篇

行銷篇

感情篇

辦公室心情隨筆

Warren:

An opening job for the operation manager is quite interesting and rare, but I think I am okay with where I am right now, as I have reasonable workloads, I have a pay that I am satisfied with, and I have tasks that I can barely handle sometimes; thus, being the operation manager should require much better abilities and suits those who work really hard for this company.

一個營運經理的職缺是蠻有趣而且珍貴的，但我想我目前這樣是可以的了，因為我有合理的工作量，有滿意的薪資，而且有時候有些任務我幾乎處理不來了，所以當一個營運經理應該會要求更好的能力，也比較適合那些很認真為公司工作的人。

Hiring someone from outside the company is unexpected, but it is acceptable since I truly believe the board has their own kind of thoughts and considerations and also they must have seen something in the new guy that they just have to hire him. We should be supportive and help this new manager to get the best out of our products and let him understand where we stand in the market and what sort of situations we had or are facing, so he can get on track quickly.

從公司外部雇用人是出乎意料但是卻可接受的，因為我真心相信董事會他們是有自己的想法和考量，而且他們一定是有看到這個新人身上的什麼點，讓他們就是想聘請他。我們應該支持且要幫助這個新的經理來透徹了解我們的產品，也讓他知道我們在市場上的定位還有我們曾經或者現在面臨的狀況，他就可以很快上手了。

Haj:

If the operation manager will leave on Monday, then I should be having a new office on Tuesday or Wednesday, I am totally going to furnish and decorate my new office to welcome this new page! Yet, John likes Warren very much, and Warren is that competent; he might be a threat to me. It would be better if I can find out whether he'll be my competitor or not. However, I work hard and they make me working day and night often, and I have never complained and have never asked for overtime pay. Also, I am good at this job and in this area. There is no doubt they would pick me for being the next operation manager.

如果營運經理禮拜一就要走了，那麼我應該在星期二或星期三就會有新辦公室了吧，我一定要裝修和佈置我的新辦公室來迎接這新的一頁！但是 John 很喜歡 Warren 而且 Warren 那麼能幹，他對我可能構成威脅。如果我能知道他是否試圖與我競爭會更好。不過，我工作認真以及他們常常讓我日以繼夜的工作，而且我從來沒抱怨過也沒有要求過要加班費。並且，在這領域裡我擅長於我的工作。毫無疑問的他們會選我當下一任的營運經理。

How come they chose that guy over me and without giving us a heads up? I really thought all my efforts, works would finally be paid off. Do I not deserve to have that title or what? Otherwise, they must have something that they are not happy about me...

為什麼他們選擇那個人而不是我，也沒有給我們個提醒？我真的以為我所有的努力終將有回報。難道我不配那個職稱嗎還是什麼？否則，他們一定有什麼事情對我不滿……

辦公室篇

貿易篇

業務篇

行銷篇

感情篇

Part 1

★ **Also what is all that hoping to "shake things up" theory...**

還有那些所有什麼希望「改革」的理論……

shake things up

整頓，在此為整頓公司之意

Or you can say:

- Company rectification.（公司整頓。）
- Re-organize the company.（重新組織公司，即也有整頓公司之意。）

★ **Actually I do not really mind having someone just parachuted into this position.**

其實我真的不介意別人就這樣空降到這個位置上。

parachute into this position

用降落傘進入這個職缺，在此為職場空降部隊之意

Or you can say:

- Get this position through connections.（靠關係得到此職缺。）
- Pull some strings for you/ Pull a few strings for you.（為你牽線／拉關係。）

★ **Time will tell.**

時間會說話。（時間會證明之意）

Or you can say:

- Truth is the daughter of time.

真理是時間的女兒。（時間見真理之意）

- Time is the best witness.

時間是最佳的證人。（時間能證明之意）

⭐ 心理小測試

滿是鏡子的房間

Q 假如今天你進入一個擁有滿是鏡子的房間裡面，那麼這時你觀察著周圍，你會發現：

A：可以看到很遠的地方以及有幾位旅客

B：周圍的不遠處就有幾位旅客

C：除了自己以外，一個人也沒有

D：周圍聚集著很多人

測驗結果
請見下頁

23

測 驗 結 果

A：你把自我與他人的界線定位的很清楚，也很注重去保留自己的空間。同時你也是一個理性且凡事注重合理的人。你也相當看重自己的知識和思考能力，旁人是無法輕易左右你的意見的。是屬於自我意識與他人意識明確型。你拿捏自己與人之間的界線拿捏得很好，所以請繼續保持吧！

B：你對於自我的觀念不是太明確，有些時候會意識不到自己自我意識所佔的比重，因此算是容易受到他人影響的。是屬於保留自我意識的人。有些時候還是應該要對自己的意見有所保留哦！

C：你的心思完完全全被自我意識所佔領，你習慣了以自我為中心，所以其他人事物對你而言都引不起你多大的興趣，更很難轉移你的注意力。是屬於極端自我中心者。你應該適當調節自己的心態，去明白：除了自己之外，其他人事物也是值得注意的。

D：你很害怕獨處也對人際關係過分依賴，也非常容易讓旁人左右你的意見。是屬於較缺乏自我意識的人。你應該試著學會認同自己，並且學著自己做主。

心理知識補一補

◇◇ Big Five 五大人格特質（Big Five personality traits）

　　McCare 以及 Costa 區分了五大人格特質（Five factor model, FFM），是現今所被廣泛接受的，此五大人格特質也簡稱 Big Five 或後來也有人以 OCEAN 稱之以方便記憶。

1. **Openness**（開放性）：好奇心、較具彈性、有豐富的想像力、有藝術家的敏感以及不墨守成規的態度。也有著創意、理智，以及可獨立思考特質的性格因素。
2. **Conscientiousness**（嚴謹性／謹慎性）：偏向於此性格的人，通常較勤奮、規律、計畫周詳、守時且較可靠，也有著控制衝動行為的能力、謹慎勤勉的行為。
3. **Extraversion**（外向性）：偏向於此性格的人，直率、喜歡社交、生氣勃勃、有自信且合群。
4. **Agreeableness**（友善性）：有同情心、值得信任、較合群、謙虛且正直，且重視與他人的和諧關係。
5. **Neuroticism**（神經質）：容易焦慮、具有敵意、自我意識較高、容易有不安全感、脆弱易受傷，容易悲傷苦惱、過度的緊迫，以及在壓力易導致適應不良。

Unit 3 給我給我！給我團購！

前情提要

Wendy is browsing a group buying website in the office during the lunch break, and she tries to convince her colleague to purchase a product together。

Wendy 在辦公室裡趁午休時間在瀏覽一個團購網站，她試著想說服她的同事一起買一個產品。

角色介紹

Wendy- a staff who initiates a team buying; a team buying initiator （一個發起了一項團購的員工–團購發起人）

Peggy- Wendy's colleague and also a team buyer（Wendy 的同事，也是參與團購的人）

情境對話

Wendy: Peggy, look! Here is a Lash and Brow Enhancing Serum, it says to grow and strengthen your lashes within 7 days only.

Peggy，妳看！這裡有一個眉睫生長液，她說只要 7 天就可以增長和強韌妳的睫毛。

Peggy: Seriously? That is so cool, because all other enhancing serums need

真的嗎？那太酷了吧，因為所有其他的生長液都至

like at least 2 weeks to see any results.

少需要 2 個禮拜才會有任何效果。

Where is it made? Is it safe without any side effects? How much is it?

它是哪裡產的？它是安全無副作用的嗎？它多少錢啊？

Wendy: It looks real and reliable, it is from Japan and I am sure their good QA is well-known, and it states that this is clinically tested.

它看起來真是可靠，它是來自日本的，而且我相信他們的優良品質保證是眾所皆知的，而且這裡還有寫這是經臨床測試過的。

We need up to 20 people for a special price of NT299 per this enhancing serum plus getting free 10 packs of eye masks per person. Otherwise, it is one for NT499 and without any free gifts. Are you interested in buying this with me or not?

要 20 人以上訂購才會有 1 支生長液加 10 包免費眼膜一套只要台幣 299 的優惠價。否則就是一支台幣 499 且也沒有任何贈品。妳有沒有興趣跟我一起買這個？

Peggy: Yes, I am. The deal sounds perfect, **count me in** and let us find other 18 people to get this special offer.

我有啊，這個優惠聽起來太讚了，算我一份，且我們再找其他 18 人來一起得到這個優惠。

辦公室篇

貿易篇

業務篇

行銷篇

感情篇

Part 1

 前情提要

Wendy and Peggy aim to have 18 peoples to join their group buying from the office, but this product cause some arguments.

Wendy 和 Peggy 目標要從辦公室裡找 18 個人來參與她們的團購，但是這個產品引發一些爭論。

 角色介紹

Wendy- a staff who initiates a team buying; a team buying initiator
（一個發起了一項團購的員工–團購發起人）

Peggy- Wendy's colleague and also a team buyer（Wendy 的同事，也是參與團購的人）

Amelia- Wendy's another colleague and holds different opinions toward this team buying product（Wendy 的另一個同事，且對於這團購商品持有不同的看法）

💬 **情境對話**

Wendy: Does anyone in here want to buy a Lash and Brow Enhancing Serum with me and Peggy? We need to find 18 more people for the deal.

這裡有任何人要跟我還有 Peggy 一起買眉睫增長液嗎？為了這個優惠我們還需要找 18 個人。

You can come and check out this website, and there is even an introduction video here. Let me know if you are interested!

你們可以來看看這個網站，甚至還有一個介紹的影片。有興趣的話讓我知道哦！

Peggy: Yes, it looks good, and it comes with freebies as well; thus, the value is definitely beyond its price.

對啊，它看起來不錯而且還有贈品，因此絕對是物超所值的。

Amelia: I have tried something like this, and I did experience dryness and itching around my eyes when I wore it during the day at that time.

我曾試過像這類的產品，那時在白天使用的時候，我的眼周會出現乾癢的症狀。

Wendy: There are plenty of similar products out there, but this one is different, and also this should only to be used at nights, didn't you know that?

外面有很多類似的產品，但這個是不同的，而且這應該在晚上才能使用，妳之前不知道嗎？

Amelia: Anyway I do not suggest anyone to buy this, **you'd better call this team buying off if you cannot guarantee us for its safety and results.**

反正我不建議任何人買這個，如果妳不能向我們保證它的安全性和效果的話，妳最好取消這個團購。

Wendy: I do not want to argue this with you, if anyone else except Amelia is interested in getting this, please let me know before 3pm.

我不想和妳爭論這個，如果任何除了 Amelia 之外的人有興趣的話，請在下午 3 點前讓我知道。

Part 1

 辦公室心情隨筆

 Wendy:

What! A Lash and Brow Enhancing Serum, and it says to grow and strengthen your lashes in only 7 days! It looks so cool and real, and to have results in such a short time, I just must get it! I want to be the first ones to try it! This special offer need 20 people to get the special price, so I must share this with others and let them know how amazing this thing is!

什麼！一個眉睫生長液，而且宣稱只要 7 天就可以增長和強韌妳的睫毛！看起來很酷也很逼真，而且這麼短時間就可以有效果，我必須得到！我想當第一批試用它的人！這個特殊優惠需要 20 個人才可以得到這個優惠價，那我必須跟其他人分享這個，而且讓她們知道這個東西有多驚人！

Okay, now Peggy is with me, now we just need 18 more people, so we can get this deal! Amelia is against this, but it is okay because she did not use it right, and it is not the same product, this one is new and different. I will just wait for others to join us then, after they watch the introduction video I am sure they will be on my side as this video is very convincing.

好，現在 Peggy 站在我這邊了，現在我們只需要再 18 個人我們就可以得到這個優惠了！Amelia 反對這個，但是沒關係，那是因為她之前沒有正確使用，而且也不是一模一樣的產品，這是一個完全不同的新產品，我只要等其他人加入我們就好了，等她們看過介紹影片後，我確定她們會站在我這邊的，因為這個影片非常有說服力。

Amelia:

What are Wendy and Peggy doing? A Lash and Brow Enhancing Serum? Come on! I have tried something like that before, and I still remember it did not work and it made me so uncomfortable during the day. It made my eyes dry and itchy for those days. I have to let everyone know because it might be not safe. They are only recommending that to everyone because they want us to join their group buying, but how can they be sure that the product is 100% safe?

Wendy 和 Peggy 在做什麼啊？一個眉睫生長液？拜託！我之前有試過像這樣的東西，而且我還記得它沒有效，還讓我白天時非常不舒服。那些天它讓我眼睛乾又癢。我必須讓大家知道因為它也許不安全。因為她們想我們加入她們團購所以她們才推薦給大家，但是她們怎們能確定產品是百分百安全呢？

Wendy said I used it wrongly so that was why I felt uncomfortable for such things, but still, they cannot guarantee for the product's safety, and how would they know if it can really work? I have to let everyone know it is not safe and they cannot buy this product with them, as I have tried so I know I cannot put everyone in danger.

Wendy 說是我使用錯誤了才會讓我對於這樣的東西不舒服，但是還是一樣，她們不能保證產品的安全性，而且她們怎麼知道它真的會有效果？我必須讓大家知道這個是不安全的，而且他們不能跟她們買這個產品，因為我有試過所以我不能讓大家處於危險之中。

好好用句型

★ **Count me in.**

算我一份

> Or you can say:

- am in.

  我加入。（也有算我一份之意）

- Add me in.

  算我一份。

★ **You'd better call this team buying off.**

妳最好取消這個團購。

call this off

將此取消，**call Off**（取消）

> Or you can say:

- Cancel this.

  取消這個。

- Pull the plug.

  終止/結束/取消。（尤其為「取消」金錢方面投資或開發案等事宜）

★ **If you cannot guarantee us for its safety and results.**

如果妳不能向我們保證它的安全性和效果。

You cannot guarantee.

你不能保證。

> Or you can say:

- You cannot assure.

  你不能保證／你不能確保。

- You cannot give your word.
  你不能給我保證。

⭐ 心理小測試

受他人影響的程度

Q 你是個能夠出於泥而不染的人嗎？你是一個容易受他人影響的人嗎？現在請你用以下四個條件畫一幅畫：

A：房子
B：樹木
C：池塘
D：路人

測驗結果
請見下頁

辦公室篇

貿易篇

業務篇

行銷篇

感情篇

測驗結果

A：在你畫的圖上，人比樹木和房子大。你容易受溫和且女性化的人影響，而強勢的人卻不容易能影響你。你崇尚美感，是一個浪漫的人。

B：在你畫的圖上，房子和樹木都大，但是人小。率直是你的魅力，你服於理論且深愛知性的事物，是個不易被感情左右的人。

C：在你畫的圖上，人比房子小，但是比樹木大。你的個性強勢不容易受影響，在逆境中常常能顯示優點，勇敢做決定且走自己的路。

D：以上皆非。你是一個只要碰到同類型的人，就可以馬上把對方同化而使彼此更親近更了解的人。但同樣的，你的生活也與某個人互相維繫著。

心理知識補一補

性格形態學

性格形態學（Enneagram of Personality）其中 "ennea" 是希臘文之中「九」的意思，而 "Enneagram" 原意是一個有九個方位的圖形。那九個方位代表九種人格，現今很多企業在員工入職前會要求做九行人格的測驗，

第一型人格–完美主義者（The Reformer）：完美、改進型、捍衛原則、秩序大使、正確主義型。

第二型人格–古道熱腸者（The Helper）：成就他人、助人、博愛、愛心大使。

第三型人格–成就追求者（The Achiever）：成就主義、實踐、實幹。

第四型人格–個人風格者（The Individualist）：浪漫、藝術、自我、多感。

第五型人格–博學多聞者（The Investigator）：觀察、思考、理智。

第六型人格–謹慎忠誠者（The Loyalist）：尋求安全、謹慎、忠誠、疑惑。

第七型人格–享樂主義者（The Enthusiast）：創造可能、活躍、享樂。

第八型人格–天生領導者（The Challenger）：挑戰、權威、領袖、指揮。

第九型人格–和平主義者（The Peacemaker）：維持和諧、和諧、平淡。

辦公室篇

貿易篇

業務篇

行銷篇

感情篇

Unit 4 魔鬼訓練

 前情提要

Mary was hired as a manager's secretary and she was told that she only needs to translate emails and interpret conversations between the company and its clients and sales agent and also some database maintaining. However recently, her boss started to request her for many more of other unexpected assignments and tasks.

Many 被雇用為經理秘書，而她當初所被告知的工作內容只是翻譯 email 以及翻譯公司和客戶還有公司和銷售商的對話，以及一些資料庫維護。然而最近她的老闆開始對她要求了其他更多的預料外的工作以及任務。

 角色介紹

Jamie- Mary's boss（Mary 的老闆）
Mary- Jamie's secretary（Jamie 的秘書）

 情境對話

Jamie: Mary, we are about to sign a sales contract with our new sales agent, since you might have some free time these days…

Mary，我們即將要與我們的一個新的銷售代理簽合約，既然妳這幾天應該會有空……

We used to pay our lawyer for

我們以前都付錢給我們的

translations, but can you translate the whole contract and give it to me by the end of the week?

律師去翻譯合約，但是妳能翻譯整份合約，然後這週結束前給我嗎？

Mary: I do not know any law term at all and there are 40 pages… I am not so sure if I can finish it. Can I have some help from our lawyer?

我完全不知道任何法律名詞而且有 40 頁……我不確定我可以完成它。我可以讓我們的律師協助我一些嗎？

Jamie: If you do not know any words you can always "Google" it, and I hope you can finish this by yourself, asking our lawyer might incur cost.

如果妳有不知道的字，妳隨時可以「Google 一下」，且我希望妳能自己完成這個，要求我們的律師幫忙可能會要花錢。

Mary: Okay, I will try my best.

好，我會盡力。

Jamie: Before that, you can go downstairs and help the engineers test our machines and better if you can memorize our 152 types of screws.

在那之前，妳可以去樓下幫工程師們測試機器，如果可以記住我們的 152 種螺絲會更好。

Also, later please use the latest iPhone 6 of yours to take some pictures and videos of our under developing products to show to clients.

還有，等等請妳用妳最新的 iPhone 6 來幫我們開發中的產品拍些照片跟影片給客戶看。

Mary: Okay.

好。

Part 1

 前情提要

Mary is complaining her recent work and assignments with her colleague.

Mary 在和她的同事抱怨她最近的工作和任務。

 角色介紹

Mary- Jamie's secretary（Jamie 的秘書）

Kevin- a colleague and also the good friend of Mary（Mary 的同事也是她的好朋友）

 情境對話

Mary: **Jamie almost drives me crazy!** She made me do works that I was not supposed to do. **I did not sign up for all these!**

Jamie 快把我給逼瘋了！她讓我做我本不該做的事。這些不是我原本想要的！

She hired me for translations only, but now I have to deal with the machines, and touch the dirty screws and there are 152 types of them.

她聘請我只是要翻譯，但我現在必須應付機械還要碰髒的螺絲，況且還有 152 種螺絲。

Mary: Moreover, she is saving money from the contract translation, so she asked me to do it.

此外，她為了省下合約翻譯的錢就叫我翻。

Kevin: Yeah, I have noticed all that, and heard she often asked you to use your phone to take pictures and videos.

對，我有注意到那些，還聽到她常叫妳用妳手機拍照片影片的。

38

Mary: Yes, that too. I do not have the responsibility to provide my personal phone for company use; it is fine if it only happens one time.

對，那個也是。我沒有義務提供個人手機給公司使用，如果只發生一次就算了。

Kevin: Perhaps you should find a chance to tell Jamie all your thoughts, try to communicate with her so she knows how you feel.

也許妳該找個機會告訴 Jamie 妳所有的想法，試著和她溝通讓她知道妳的感受。

In the meantime, you should find a way to relax yourself. You are too stressed and you seem tense.

在這期間，妳應該要找到個方法來放鬆自己，妳壓力太大也太壓迫了。

辦公室心情隨筆

Mary:

I am pretty sure that I did not come here for these chores. I was not informed that I should be doing our lawyer's works. It is not like I ever studied law, and if Jamie is saving that law translation fee from lawyers, with contents that much, shouldn't she pay me some extra work fee for this? She should not ask me to do these things and act like she is right to do so. Besides, translating law documents is already a lot to ask. Now she is having me taking pictures and videos through my personal phone? Even if she needs my help to photograph, she should provide me a company phone for that use. Now more ridiculously, she wants me to test the machines and deal with the mechanism stuffs, how is that even my area? All these things are not acceptable and inappropriate, but Jamie is making me so hard to say "no" to and she leaves me no choice.

我蠻確定我不是來這裡做這些雜事的。我並沒有被告知要做我們律師的工作，又不是說我是讀法律的，而且如果 Jamie 要從律師那裡省下法律翻譯費，這麼多的內容，她不應該付我些額外工作費用嗎？她不應該叫我做這些事然後還一副她這樣做是沒錯的樣子。再說，翻譯法律文件已經很過份了。現在她還要我用我個人的手機拍照和錄影？就算她需要我幫忙攝影，她應該要提供給我一支公司電話來那樣使用。現在更荒謬的，她要我去幫忙測試機器，然後處理那些機械的事情，那又是我的領域了嗎？所有這些事情都是不可接受的也是不正當的，但是 Jamie 讓我很難說「不」，而且她讓我沒有選擇的餘地。

Telling Kevin makes me feel much better, and it is good that Kevin gets me and knowing he is on my side. He is correct, I need to find a way to release my stress.

告訴 Kevin 讓我感覺好多了，而且 Kevin 懂我還有知道他是站在我這邊的，真好。他說的對，我需要找個方法來釋放我的壓力。

Jamie:

It is close to sign up the new contract, but the contract is all in English we need some translations. Normally, we pay our lawyers for contract translation, but since Mary now looks free and might have time for this for the next few days, why don't I just ask Mary then? She was not majored in law, but it is all translations. If she finds any law term that she does not know, she can use google to help her. It should not be that hard. Besides, translations are the reasons why we hired her for. Mary can learn to test our machines as well because she seems quite free now. She then can know more about our products. For all our under developing products, I hope they can be recorded by taking pictures of them, and she's got a good phone, why not ask her to take pictures and even better she can record some videos on the products. I think it is okay to have Mary do these things because I do not want her to have nothing to do here.

　　快要到簽新合約的時候了，但是合約都是英文我們需要些翻譯。通常我們是付我們律師錢去翻譯合約，但是既然 Mary 現在有空而且接下來幾天也可能有時間，我幹嘛不叫 Mary 做就好了？她不是主修法律的，但是都是翻譯。如果她發現有法律術語她不知道的話，她可以用 google 幫助她。這應該不會是太難的。再說，我們僱用她就是為了翻譯啊。如果 Mary 現在看起來蠻空閒的，也可以來學著幫我們測試產品。對於所有我們開發中的產品，我希望它們可以以拍照的方式被記錄，我看 Mary 有個好手機，何不叫她來拍照。可以替產品錄影的話甚至是更

Part 1

好。我認為叫 Mary 做這些事情是可以的，因為我不想她在這裡沒事情做。

好好用句型

★ **Jamie almost drives me crazy!**
Jamie 快把我給逼瘋了！
Drive me crazy.
把我逼瘋。

Or you can say:

- Drive me nuts.
  把我逼瘋。
- Drive me out of my wits.
  讓我失去理智。（即有把我逼瘋之意）

★ **I did not sign up for all these!**
這些不是我原本想要的！
This is not what I sign up for.
這不是我原本想要的。（通常指事情）

Or you can say:

- I did not ask for this.
  這不是我要的。（可指事情或物品）
- This is not what I wanted in the first place.
  這不是我原先想要的。（可指事或物）

★ **In the meantime, you should find a way to relax yourself, you are too stressed and you seem tense.**
在這期間，妳應該要找到個方法來放鬆自己，妳壓力太大也太壓迫了。

in the meantime / at the meantime 在這期間/與此同時

- Meanwhile, …

  在同時間……（指同時間但卻不同地點，例如當 A 在家寫功課，B 在網咖上網）

- At the same time…

  在同時……

 心理小測試

職場抗壓性

Q 如果你要參加一個運動社團，你會偏好參加以下哪個社團：

A：打籃球

B：打壁球

C：打排球

測驗結果
請見下頁

43

測驗結果

A：選擇打籃球的你，你的抗壓指數高達 99%。你是一個抗壓高手，是個懂得將壓力轉為助力的人。當壓力來臨時，你很會排解壓力也會把壓力轉換掉。

B：選擇打壁球的你，你的抗壓指數為 65%。你有一定的企圖心，但是抗壓性不夠強。你是個遇到壓力會替自己找出口宣洩的人。你對自己的要求頗高，會朝著自己的目標努力前進，雖然會遇到挫敗的事情讓你覺得壓力很大，甚至想逃跑，但你都還能堅持下去。

C：選擇打排球的你，你的抗壓指數為 20%。你認為，在職場上不需要硬碰硬，只要把自己的事情做好就好。如果一些太超過的壓力來臨，你會覺得忍忍就好，不需要跟對方爭。但是，當壓力過高時，你會想選擇逃跑甚至一走了之。

心理知識補一補

◇◇ 完美主義者 vs 天生領導者

完美主義型（Reformer/Perfectionist）：對話中的Mary可被歸類為一個完美主義者

基本欲望：希望自己是對的、好的、貞潔的、有誠信的

對自己的要求：只要我做得對就好了。

特質：世界是黑白分明的，對是對，錯是錯；做人一定要公正；做事一定要有效率。

處理感情的方法：(1) 壓抑，否定

　　　　　　　　　 (2) 追求完美，討厭不守規則的人。

常用辭彙：應該、不應該；對、錯；不、不是的；照規矩。

天生領導者（Leader）：對話中的Jamie性格偏向於是一個支配者

基本欲望：決定自己在生命中的方向，做強者。

對世界的要求：堅強及能夠控制自己的處境就好了。

特質：徹底的自由主義者，是掌舵人、創業者，好戰。

處理感情的方法：(1) 喜歡控制別人照自己的方式做，怕別人閒著

　　　　　　　　　 (2) 對人防衛性強，防止自己受傷。

常用辭彙：喂，你…；我告訴你…；為什麼不能？；就…就好了。

Part 1

Unit 5 打造完美的辦公環境

 前情提要

Garrett is in the office asking his colleagues if they might need any new office supplies and equipment.

Garrett 在辦公室裡問他的同事或許是否有需要任何新辦公室用品和設備

 角色介紹

Garrett- responsible for asking his colleagues for requests of new office supplies and equipment（負責向他的同事詢問新辦公室用品和設備的要求）

Jeff- a colleague of Garrett（Garrett 的一個同事）

 情境對話

Garrett: Laurie from the Purchasing Department is asking us to fill up this Office Supply Request Form before the end of the month.

採購部的 Laurie 要求我們在月底前要填寫此辦公室用品申請表。

They informed us to only request necessary supplies or equipment as they have a lower budget this year.

他們通知我們只能要求必要的物資和設備，因為他們今年預算比較低。

Garrett: I think all sorts of stationaries in

我認為各種在供應室的文

the supply room are still quite enough for us to use for years.

具還相當足夠我們用好幾年。

Jeff: We do have plenty of spare ones, but can some of them be replaced? I am thinking to have ergonomic keyboards and mice for us.

我們是有很多備品，但是有些可以被取代嗎？我在想的是可以給我們有符合人體工學的鍵盤和滑鼠。

About 60 percent of our employees reported hand or arm symptoms last year, mostly from tendinitis and due to typing and clicking nonstop.

大約有 60%的員工報告出現了手或手臂的症狀，大多是因為無止盡的打字和點擊而引起的肌腱炎。

The ergonomic keyboards and mice can not only reduce their pain, but also help decrease the number of employees suffering from tendinitis.

符合人體工學的鍵盤和滑鼠，不僅可以減輕他們的痛苦，也有利於減少受肌腱炎之苦的員工的數量。

Garrett: That makes sense, thank you Jeff. I will ensure to put these down in the form.

這是有道理的，Jeff 謝謝你。我會確保把這些在表格裡寫下來。

Part 1

 前情提要

Garrett continues to collect opinions from his colleagues toward the purchasing of new office supplies and equipment.

Garrett 繼續收集他的同事關於新辦公室用品與設備採買的意見。

 角色介紹

Garrett- responsible for asking his colleagues for requests of new office supplies and equipment（負責向他的同事詢問新辦公室用品和設備的要求）

Jeff, Douglas, Gregory- the colleague of Garrett（Garrett 的同事們）

 情境對話

Garrett: Do we have any other purchasing suggestions from anyone for the office?

任何人對於辦公室還有其他購買建議嗎？

Douglas: Can we get new office chairs as well? These ones are uncomfortable. I have sore backs because of it.

我們可以也得到新辦公椅嗎？這些不舒服。我背部酸痛就是因為它。

Gregory: Yes they are, and if it is possible that we are allowed to get a new coffee machine? The automated one makes good coffee and saves time.

對啊，還有，我們可以被允許得到一個新的咖啡機嗎？自動化的那種，可以泡出好咖啡也節省時間。

Jeff: New chairs are needed, but automated coffee machines I am not so sure.

是需要新椅子的，但是自動咖啡機我就不確定了。

Gregory: A cup of good coffee in the morning is essential and time is money.

早上一杯好咖啡是必要的，而且時間就是金錢。

Jeff: Automated does not equal to good, and making a cup of coffee does not take a lot of time. How about we ask what others think?

自動的不等於是最好的，而且泡杯咖啡不會花很多時間。不如我們問問其他人怎麼想？

Gregory: You do not know coffee. Garrett what do you recommend?

你不懂咖啡。Garrett 你有什麼建議嗎？

Garrett: **Instead of buying a new automated coffee machine to spend a lot, perhaps changing coffee beans?** Gregory you can choose the beans.

也許換咖啡豆，而不是花大錢買一台新的咖啡機？ Gregory 你可以選豆子。

Jeff: **Fair enough.**

有道理。

Gregory: **That would work.**

這樣也不錯。

辦公室心情隨筆

Garrett:

I am in charge for the purchasing of new office supplies and equipment this time, I am not so sure if we need anything. From what I remember, we have plenty of spares in the supply room. Maybe, I will go ask other colleagues to check if they want anything or to see if they think we might need anything for the office. The purchasing department is having a lower budget this year, so I have to make sure reminding my colleagues about that, since they put me in charge for this, they might assume that I can assist them to keep things under control and under the budget that they have given.

我負責這次新辦公室用品與設備的採買，我不太確定我們是否有需要任何東西。 據我所記得的，我們在供應室裡有很多備品。也許我要去問問其他同事他們有沒有想要的東西，或者看看他們有沒有覺得辦公室裡需要什麼。採購部今年預算比較低，所以我要確保我提醒同事這點，因為他們讓我負責這個，他們可能認為我可以協助他們掌控事情，也控制在他們給的預算內。

Jeff is having a good point, and it is very thoughtful of him to think of those colleagues in pain, it is certain that we should act to prevent such things from happening to other colleagues.

Jeff 給了很好的建議，且他這樣想到那些在痛苦中的同事是很體貼的，我們要防止這種事情再發生到其他同事上就是必須要動作的。

New chairs are needed as well, but coffee machine I am not so sure. Automatic coffee machines and good ones usually cost a lot. However, Gregory looks quite insisted on having a good coffee every morning. How about we use better coffee beans? Let me ask them to see if this is acceptable.

新的椅子也是需要的，但是咖啡機我就不確定了。自動咖啡機還要好的通常都會要花很多錢。然而，Gregory 看起來蠻堅持每天早上要來杯好咖啡。不如我們換一個好的咖啡豆？讓我來問問他們這是否是可接受的。

Jeff:

It is the new office suppliers and equipment requests time again. Yes, Garrett is correct we have enough stock in the supply room. Though, I think I can make a suggestion on buying some ergonomic keyboards and mice for everyone. I heard that there's an increasing number of employees having hand or arm symptoms, and the company has not yet done anything about this issue yet. The ergonomic keyboards and mice should somehow reduce pain and also can reduce the possibility for employees suffering from tendinitis. Okay, I will recommend this to Garrett and see if he agrees with me.

又到了新辦公室用品與設備採買的時間了。對的，Garrett 說的沒錯，我們在供應室裡面有足夠的庫存。但是，我想我該給個建議在買些符合人體工學的鍵盤和滑鼠上面。我聽說我們員工有手或手臂的症狀的數字增加了，然後公司還沒對此問題做任何處理。這種符合人體工學的鍵盤和滑鼠應該可以多少減輕痛苦，也可以減少其他員工受肌腱炎之苦的機率。好的，我會建議 Garrett 這個然後看他是否同意我。

Douglas is right we need our chairs to be replaced, too. I have to give my support to new chairs. Why would Gregory ask for a new coffee machine when Garrett already said to buy only necessary things? Maybe he has a reason why we have to? A new coffee machine is going to cost a lot, I do not see why we must replace the old one when it is not out of order.

　　Douglas 是對的，我們也需要更換我們的椅子。我要支持新椅子的更換。為什麼 *Garrett* 已經說只買必要買的東西了，*Gregory* 還會要求一個新的咖啡機？也許他有我們要這麼做的理由？一個新的咖啡機會要花很多錢的，我不明白為什麼舊的還沒壞掉我們就要買新的。

　　Yes, buying new coffee beans is smarter and cheaper. Good on Garrett.

　　是的，買新咖啡豆聰明多了也便宜多了。*Garrett* 好樣的。

好好用句型

★ **Instead of buying a new automated coffee machine to spend a lot, perhaps changing coffee beans?**

也許換咖啡豆，而不是花大錢買一台新的咖啡機？

spend a lot 花大錢

　　Or you can say:

　　● Cost a fortune.

　　　花了一大筆錢。

　　● Cost me an arm and a leg.

　　　付出了我的一隻手臂及一條腿。（即為價值不斐，花了不少錢之意）

★ **Fair enough.**

有道理；說的對；很公平/夠公平。

　　Or you can say:

　　● That makes sense.

　　　有道理。

　　● That gets a point.

　　　這有值得給一分。（即為有道理之意）

★ **That would work.**

這樣也不錯／這樣也行得通。

Or you can say:

- That will do.

  這可以行的通。

- That is executable. / That is workable.

  這是可執行的。

 **心理小測試**

潛在願望

Q 假如你所居住的房子發生了深夜大火，而當下你只能選擇以下的其中一樣東西和你一起逃跑，你會選擇哪個：

A：時鐘／鬧鐘

B：食物

C：錢

D：衣服

E：日記或有紀念性的物品

測驗結果
請見下頁

測 驗 結 果

A：若你選擇了時鐘／鬧鐘，代表你是一個態度很積極的人，你的頭腦很靈光，工作能力也很強，只不過有時候你會有點自信過盛。

B：若你選擇了食物，則代表你是一個很樂天的人，你常常無條件的熱心助人。

C：若你選擇了錢，代表你是一個集大膽與冷靜於一身的人，凡事都能以集體利益為重，是較不會被眼前的小利所誘惑的人。

D：若你選擇了衣服，代表你是一個絕對不會魯莽行事的人，你小心謹慎，有強烈的責任感。

E：若你選擇了日記或有紀念性的物品，代表你是一個異性緣很強的人，你的感情豐富且品味超群，常常會有浪漫的際遇。

選擇 A 或 B 或 C 的人，有個共同特點就是，這三類型的人都屬於較難以拒絕別人要求的人，即使是自己做不到的事情，也不太會開口拒絕。

選擇 D 或 E 的人，你有時候會因為自己的責任感太強而產生壓力。

心理知識補一補

環境心理學

環境心理學（Environmental Psychology）是一門研究所處的環境對人的心理及行為之間會產生怎樣的影響，還有會造成怎樣的變化的應用社會心理學。

這一個領域開始被人們廣為討論的時間較晚，大約是出現在 1960 年之後。起因推測應為在當時因為人類文明的發展嚴重地影響到自然環境，還有都市化效應所帶來的人口密度增加、個人空間減少、噪音及空氣污染的問題愈來愈嚴重等。在 1980 年到 2000 年之間，這一門心理學開始蓬勃發展，被應用在許多方面，例如是土地規劃、環境保護之類的，而在生活中最常見到的就是辦公室環境的規劃。

在本單元之中，Jeff 及 Douglas 提出的是以員工生理健康層面為考量的更換符合人體工學的鍵盤滑鼠及辦公椅，以減少已知的職業傷害（occupational injury）。而 Gregory 主張更換的咖啡機雖然也是硬體設備，但 "A cup of good coffee in the morning." 卻比較像是心理層面上的需求。值得讚賞的是在對話中，員工間的簡短討論，想出了替代的方法以更換咖啡豆來滿足 Gregory 的需求，而不是以忽視員工意見或是強行否決的處理方式。這樣的話，可能就不是單純地以更換辦公室設備就能解決了！

辦公室篇

貿易篇

業務篇

行銷篇

感情篇

Part 1

Unit 6 鬼來電……

前情提要

Berry will be working late in the office tonight and her colleagues tell her about the events they experienced.

Berry 今晚要加班，然後她同事告訴她她們經歷過的事件。

角色介紹

Vinci: Staff 1（職員 1）

Mina: Staff 2（職員 2）

Berry: Staff 3（職員 3）

情境對話

Vinci: Finally, I have finished the work of the day, how about you, Mina?

終於，我完成今天的工作了，妳呢，Mina？

Mina: **I am almost there but still have not done yet, are you getting off work first?**

我快好了但是還沒好，妳要先下班了嗎？

Berry: **I think I might have to work overtime today**, guess I will be here by myself in the office then.

我想我今天可能會加班，看來我要自己在這辦公室了。

Vinci: Mina, I can wait for you if you are finishing soon, Berry, you have to be careful for getting weird calls.

Mina，如果妳快結束了我可以等妳，Berry，妳要小心接到怪電話。

Vinci: Sometimes, I get nuisance calls, while I work late in the office, those are quite scary.

有時候我在辦公室工作到很晚的時候會接到騷擾電話，那些還蠻恐怖的。

Berry: What kind of calls and how scary? Are those prank calls from kids or what?

怎樣的電話有多恐怖？那些是小孩子的惡作劇電話還是？

Vinci: I do not know but sometimes only ring once, other times it rings more times and no one speaks when I say "Hello".

我不知道但有時只響一次，其他時候是響很多次，但是當我接起來說「哈囉」的時候沒有人出聲。

Berry: Great! Prank calls! So that means I will not be alone tonight.

很好！惡作劇電話！所以這代表我今晚不會孤獨了。

Vinci: Yes, but not in a good way, when it happens, you will find out how you wish you did not get those calls.

是的，但是是不好的那種，當它發生時妳就會知道妳有多希望妳沒接到那些電話了。

Part 1

Berry and Vinci are in the office talking about the prank calls Berry got when she worked overtime last night.

Berry 和 Vinci 在辦公室討論 Berry 昨晚加班時候接到的惡作劇電話。

 角色介紹

Vinci: Staff 1（職員 1）
Mina: Staff 2（職員 2）
Berry: Staff 3（職員 3）

 情境對話

Vinci: How was last night Berry? Did you enjoy working late here?

昨天晚上怎麼樣，Berry？妳有享受在這裡工作到很晚嗎？

Berry: Not at all, I wish you did not tell me, and I felt scared all night and could not concentrate on works at all.

一點也不，我真希望妳沒告訴我，而我整晚都感到害怕，然後都無法專心在工作上。

Vinci: Sorry, I just wanted you to be prepared, so you might be less scared when it happens. Did you get any calls? No?

對不起，我只想讓妳做好準備，然後發生的話妳比較不會害怕。妳有接到任何電話嗎？沒有嗎？

Berry: In fact, I did. Several times. After 8pm, it was like one call every 10 minutes and only rang once.

事實上我有。好幾次。晚上 8 點後，好像是每 10 分鐘一通而且只響一聲。

Vinci: Oh my god. Were you alright? I cannot imagine it.

我的天啊。妳那時還好嗎？我無法想像。

Berry: I was so terrified, but then I was more than alright, just angry.

我當時很害怕，但是後來我好到不能再好，只是生氣而已。

Berry: I picked up the last call which it kept ranging, and then I heard Mina laughing, and she confessed to make all those stupid calls last night.

最後一通電話一直響的時候我接起來了，然後我聽到 Mina 在笑，然後她承認昨晚那些愚蠢的電話都是她打的。

Vinci: You cannot be serious. Mina? So is she also responsible for all the calls I got when I worked late?

妳不是認真的吧。Mina？那我工作到很晚的時後接到的那些電話也跟她有關嗎？

Berry: Just last night as she was there when you reminded me this and **she decided to scare the hell out of me.**

只有昨天晚上，因為昨天妳提醒我這件事的時候她也在啊，然後她就決定要嚇死我。

Vinci: Very mature!

真成熟！

辦公室篇

貿易篇

業務篇

行銷篇

感情篇

Part 1

辦公室心情隨筆

 Vinci:

So good I do not have to work late today, I will see if Mina is going, too. Berry is staying late in the office, I should get her a head up about the scary prank calls that I always get when I work overtime. I guess she can be more prepared and be less scared. Looks like Berry does not really get what I mean. She will find out when she gets the calls. Better if she does not get the calls though because it freaked me out a lot.

我不用工作到很晚太好了，我來看看 Mina 是不是也要走了。Berry 要在辦公室待很晚，我應該提醒她關於我每次加班都會接到的恐怖惡作劇電話的事情，我猜她比較有心理準備的話比較不會害怕。看來 Berry 不是真的很明白我所說的意思。等她接到了就會知道了。雖然最好是她不會接到，因為這種事情總是會很嚇到我。

Let me ask Berry if she is doing alright last night.

讓我來問問看 Berry 昨晚是否還可以。

What? I reminded Berry just out of kindness I did not mean to scare her. What? Mina made these calls last night? What made her to do such an immature thing? How could she make jokes like that? That means it was not supposed to have any terrifying phone calls for Berry last night; however, because Mina heard what I said, she made that joke. Is it my fault then? I feel sorry.

什麼！我出於好意提醒 Berry，不是有意要嚇她的，可憐的 Berry。什麼？Mina 昨晚打了那些電話？是什麼原因讓她做這麼不成熟的事情？她怎麼可以開那樣的玩笑？那就代表 Berry 本來不會接到任何嚇人的電話，而是因為 Mina 聽到我說了才開那樣的玩笑。那麼這是我的錯了嗎？我覺得很抱歉。

Berry:

Looks like I will be the only one staying in the office until late tonight. Vinci said that she gets weird calls when she works late here. It sounds quite creepy being here alone at night and all in the sudden phone rings and no one speaks. Maybe it is alright, it is probably just stupid calls from children, and it is not a big deal.

看來，今晚我會是唯一一個在辦公室裡工作到很晚的人了。Vinci 說她加班的時候會接到奇怪的電話。聽起來蠻毛骨悚然的，自己獨自在這一整個晚上，然後突然電話會響起然後沒人講話。也許沒事的，這有可能只是小孩愚蠢的惡作劇電話而已，沒什麼大不了的。

I wish Vinci did not let me know about this because now I will just be scared all night wondering when the phones are going to ring though she meant well.

我寧願 Vinci 沒告訴我這件事情，因為現在我就會一整晚害怕，然後好奇著什麼時候電話會響起，雖然她是好意。

Oh, my goodness! The phone is ringing now, the phone keeps ringing non-stop. Should I pick up? Okay, I will answer the phone.

我的天啊！現在電話響了，電話不停的響。我該接起來嗎？好吧，我會接起來。

What? Isn't that Mina's voice? This sounds so like Mina and she is laughing. This is so not funny.

什麼？這不是 Mina 的聲音嗎？這聽起來好像 Mina 而且她還在笑。這一點都不好笑。

Vinci wonders how my night was, I got to tell her what Mina did yesterday and I have to tell her how terrified I was last night. I am also telling her how much I wish she did not *tell me, so I did not have to go through all that.*

Vinci 好奇我昨晚怎麼樣，我一定要告訴她 Mina 昨天做了什麼，我還要告訴她我昨天晚上有多被嚇到。我也要告訴她我多麼希望她沒有告訴我，我就不用經歷那些。

 好好用句型

★ **I am almost there, but still have not done yet, are you getting off work first?**

我快好了，但是還沒好，妳要先下班了嗎？

get off work

下班

　　Or you can say:

- Get off duty.

　下班。

- Clock out. / Punch out.

　打卡下班。

★ **I think I might have to work overtime today.**

我想我今天可能會加班。

work overtime

加班

　　Or you can say:

- Work extra hours.

　上多的時數。（則有加班之意）

- Work extra shifts.

　加班。（用在有輪班的工作，例如醫院和便利商店）

★ **She decided to scare the hell out of me.**
她就決定要嚇死我。
Scare the hell out of me! 嚇死我！
　Or you can say:
- I was nearly dead with fright.
　我差一點被嚇到往生！
- You freaked me out.
　你嚇到我了！

心理小測試

幼稚指數

Q 假如，你今天是知名童話故事中想吃掉小紅帽的大野狼，你覺得以下哪種方法是可以讓你最順利吃掉小紅帽的？

A：用槌子把門砸壞，然後進到屋裡吃掉小紅帽

B：等小紅帽自己沒戒心的走出來，然後吃掉小紅帽

C：模仿小紅帽外婆的聲音，騙她開門後吃掉她

D：從煙囪偷偷爬進屋裡，然後吃掉小紅帽

E：用煙燻小紅帽，讓她暈倒後吃掉她

辦公室篇

貿易篇

業務篇

行銷篇

感情篇

測驗結果

A：你的幼稚指數為 **80%**。這類型的人比較大男人主義或者大女人主義，你的外表也許看起來是成熟的，但是內心卻非常幼稚。

B：你的幼稚指數為 **20%**。你是深知「強扭的瓜不甜」的道理的人，對於很多事情都懂得放手與放下。因此，你首先會選擇用等待的方式來做很多事情，無論在愛情或者工作上都是。

C：你的幼稚指數為 **40%**。此類型的人擅於用言語與人溝通，因此，在處理事情的時候，你是很有耐心且較能夠抓住人心和人性的。

D：你的幼稚指數為 **55%**。此類型的人懂的善用方法做事情，在人生的路途中能不斷的學習，是個會讓自己在不斷摸索的過程中學習成長的人。

E：你的幼稚指數為 **99%**。此類型的人喜歡憑著自己的感覺走，想做什麼就立刻做，是屬於比較長不大的類型。

心理知識補一補

恐懼

　　有時候，人會產生一種莫名其妙的恐懼（Fear），會感到忐忑不安。這種現象發展到嚴重時，當事者會自感心神不定，坐立不安，焦躁煩悶，甚至陷入不能自拔的痛苦境地，也會由此而引起血壓升高，心跳加快，食欲減退和頭痛失眠。恐懼是一種較輕的心理或精神障礙，但還不是精神病。恐懼可以表現在日常生活的各個方面，常見的如：對鬼怪的恐懼，對疾病的恐懼，或對食物的恐懼等。在心理學上認為世界上並沒有鬼神，這實際上是由心理學上所說的錯覺和幻覺所造成。

　　特殊恐懼症（specific phobia）是個人於對若干特殊類型的物體或情境感到恐懼。此恐懼局限於特定場合，如怕接近某種特殊動物、怕高（懼高症–acrophobia）、怕雷電、怕黑暗、怕飛行、怕封閉的空間（幽閉恐懼症–claustrophobia）、怕使用公共廁所、怕吃某種食物、怕牙醫、怕見血。雖然誘發因素各不相同，但與之接觸就能引發其驚恐發作。

辦公室篇

貿易篇

業務篇

行銷篇

感情篇

Part 2
貿易篇

Unit 1 給我報價

 前情提要

Rosemary is calling from the office requesting quotations for keyboards from Steve- the seller.

Rosemary 從辦公室打去給 Steve－賣家，要求鍵盤的報價。

 角色介紹

Rosemary- Buyer from GT Corp.（GT 公司的買家）

Steve- Seller （supplier） of keyboards（鍵盤的賣家－供應商）

 情境對話

Rosemary: Hi, this is Rosemary calling from GT Corp. and I am looking for PS2 mini keyboards with 85 keys.

嗨，我是從 GT 公司打來的 Rosemary，我在找 85 鍵的 PS2 迷你鍵盤。

Steve: Hi this is Steve, we now have a special price for 88 keys ones, would you like to consider it instead?

嗨，我是 Steve，我們現在 88 鍵的有特價，妳要不要乾脆考慮它？

Rosemary: Thank you, Steve, but our clients prefer the size of the 85 keys.

謝謝你，Steve，但是我們的客戶更喜歡 85 鍵的尺寸。

I am interested in this ID number SKU0037 from your catalog; may you provide us a quotation for a quantity of 100 pcs?

我所感興趣的是你們目錄上的這個 ID 號碼 SKU0037，你可以為我們提供一個數量為 100 個的報價嗎？

Steve: For SKU0037, it is NT200 per piece and now its minimum order quantity is 300 pieces, by the way, we do have quantity discounts for larger orders.

SKU0037 的話是每件台幣 200 元，然後現在的最小訂購量為 300 件，對了，較大的訂單有數量上的折扣。

Thus, if you could increase the quantity to 600 pcs, the price would only be NT150 per keyboard.

因此如果妳能增加數量到 600 個，每個鍵盤的價格會只有台幣 150 元。

Rosemary: 600 pcs is a bit too much, but I will consider it since it is way cheaper, please email me your quotation, and I will get back to you. You still have my email address, right?

600 個有點太多了，但我會考慮，因為它便宜太多了，請 email 給我你的報價然後我會再回覆你。你還有我的電子郵件地址，對嗎？

Steve: Yes, I do. I will send you the quotation by noon.

是的，我有。我會在中午前寄報價給妳。

辦公室篇
貿易篇
業務篇
行銷篇
感情篇

Part 2

前情提要

Steve is calling to follow up toward his quotation given to Rosemary.

Steve 打去跟進他提供給 Rosemary 的報價。

角色介紹

Rosemary- Buyer from GT Corp.（GT 公司的買家）

Steve- Seller（supplier） of keyboards（鍵盤的賣家–供應商）

情境對話

Steve: Hi Rosemary, **this is Steve calling to follow up your decision on keyboard's quotation.**

嗨，Rosemary，我是 Steve 打來跟進妳對於鍵盤報價的決定。

Rosemary: Hi Steve, yeah… about that…, we kind of have pressure toward the quantities, you see we do not have the quantity needed even for your minimum order quantity let alone reach to the quantity for discounts.

嗨，Steve，嗯……關於那個……，我們對於數量方面有點壓力，即使是達到你的最低訂購量的數量需求，我們都有困難，更不用說要達到可以折扣的數量了。

Steve: Well… rules are rules; can't you just purchase 600 pcs and leave the rest as spare stocks?

這個嘛……規定就是規定，難道妳們就不能買 600 個，然後剩下的當庫存嗎？

Rosemary: Steve, you have to understand

Steve 你要了解我們是一

we are a very small company without stable orders and we change and update our machines often, so we might not require the same keyboards, keeping spares is really unnecessary and not smart. Is it possible for you to let us order 200 pcs but with a lower price, so I can better report to my manager?

個非常小型、沒有穩定訂單的公司，然後我們常常改變或更新我們的機器，所以我們不一定會需要同樣的鍵盤。留著當備用真的是沒必要，也不明智。有沒有可能你能讓我們訂購 200 個，但以更低一點的價格，這樣我比較好可以跟我的主管報告？

Steve: **It is not negotiable.**

這是沒有商量的餘地的。

Rosemary: Or can you please kindly give us some discounts if we make it 300 pcs?

或者如果我們訂購 300 個，可以好心給我們一些折扣嗎？

Steve: Sorry, it is not negotiable. The offer I sent you stays the same, and it is valid for 7 days. If we do not receive your purchase order by then, **we will be looking forward to working with you next time.**

抱歉，這是沒得商量的。我給妳的報價維持不變，而且有效期為 7 天。如果我們到時候沒有收到你們的訂單，我們就會期待著與妳下一次的合作。

Rosemary: Okay, I get that, thank you.

好吧，我懂了，謝謝。

Part 2

辦公室心情隨筆

 Rosemary:

This company has the keyboards that our client wants, but we only need a small amount. I don't know if they would accept it. I will call and ask for a quotation first.

這家公司有我們客戶要的鍵盤，但我們只需要小數量，我不知道他們會不會接受。我會先打去要個報價。

The quantity discount seems nice but we really do not need that much keyboards since we have done business with them before, maybe there is still a chance for us to ask for discount with small quantity or a special price. I hope he will understand.

這個數量折扣看起來不錯，但是我們真的不需要那麼多鍵盤，因為我們之前有跟他們做過生意，也許我們還有機會要求降低可折扣的數量，或者一個特別的價格。我希望他會明白。

Now he is calling to follow up, I'd better spit the truth and let him know our difficulties. I just need to explain to him our company's problem, and I think he will then be convinced.

現在他打來要跟進了，我最好快吐出事實，讓他知道我們的難處。我只需要向他解釋我們公司的問題，然後我想他就會被說服了。

He is not buying our story; he does not listen at all. When they were still a small company, they used to beg us for orders and now they run the business well, they just decide to ignore our small orders. I am not going to show that I am mad, I will keep asking for possibilities and see how it goes.

他不相信我們的說法，他完全不聽。當他們還是小公司的時候，他們都求我們給他們訂單，然後現在他們生意做得不錯了，就決定忽略我們的小訂單。我不會讓他知道我生氣了，我會繼續詢問可能性然後看怎

72

麼樣。

He is not open for any discussions, okay, I will see what to do or check with other companies.

他不開放任何討論空間，好吧，我會看看我能做什麼，或者看看其他公司。

Steve:

Rosemary is calling for keyboards now. I have to tell her we do not do small orders now. I will need to tell her our minimum order quantity so she will get it. I will also let her know our quantity discounts and hopefully they are smart enough to pick the right offer.

Rosemary 現在為了鍵盤打來，我要告訴她我們現在不做小訂單了，我會需要告訴她我們的最小訂購量，那她就會明白了。我也會讓她知道我們的折扣數量，然後希望他們夠聰明，會選擇對的提案。

The quantity discounts sounds attractive, why does she still need to think about it? After all these years, are they still going to give me small orders only? I will call her in the afternoon to follow up.

這個折扣數量聽起來很誘人，為什麼她還會需要想想？這麼多年了，他們還仍然要只給我小訂單嗎？我下午再打給她跟進一下。

Now, I will call her to see if they are buying the product or what. Okay, now she is giving excuses for discounts. I am not breaking the rules just for her as they do not give many orders and always small orders. It is not like they do not have money for purchasing the spare ones. This conversation should be ended; there's no point for me to keep listening to her. I will just give her a deadline for getting back to me and finish this *phone call. Hope her company can stick to our rules and finally give us larger orders.*

現在我要打給她，看她們有沒有要買產品，或者要怎麼樣。好，現在她要為了折扣給理由。我不要為了她打破規矩，因為他們給不多訂單而且永遠是小訂單。他們又不是說沒有錢買多餘的。這個對談該結束了，我這樣繼續聽她講下去沒有意義。我就給她一個回覆我的期限，然後結束這通電話。希望她可以遵守規定，然後能給我們大訂單。

 好好用句型

★ **This is Steve calling to follow up your decision on keyboard's quotation.**
我是 **Steve**，打來跟進你對於鍵盤報價的決定。

follow up
跟進／追蹤（通常指工作上的進度）

> Or you can say:
> - Chase up.
>   追蹤。
> - Track it.
>   跟進它。

★ **It is not negotiable.**
這是沒有商量的餘地的。

> Or you can say:
> - There is no room for discussion.
>   沒有討論的空間。
> - It is not discussable.
>   這是不可討論的。

★ **We will be looking forward to working with you next time.**
我們期待著與妳下一次的合作。

look forward to

期待。在商務用語及口語當中常會用到 look forward to，也常常會出錯，這裡要注意的是 look forward to 是一組片語動詞，所以不適用介系詞 to 後加原形動詞的規則，用法如下 look forward to + N（名詞）

- look forward to + Ving（動名詞）
  期待

 心理小測試

受他人影響的程度

Q 假如給你可以放一個月長假的時間，你會最嚮往到什麼樣的地方去生活一個月，然後去記錄當地的風土人情呢？

A：鄉村小鎮

B：現代都會

C：原始叢林

D：文化古蹟

測驗結果
請見下頁

Part 2

A：你討厭被別人誤解，若是有一天聽到了自己的不實傳聞，你會十分氣憤的將這件事情放在心上。但你不愛與別人起衝突，你也不希望自己的解釋反而讓事情有越描越黑的可能性，所以大多時候你會吞下怨氣，可是久而久之，你對於其他人的信任會日益減少。

B：你在各種環境中都能適應良好，不管問題有多棘手你都能夠處之泰然，找到適當的方法去應付。你早就已經很老練了，所以八卦流言對你而言，只不過是茶餘飯後的話題罷了。

C：你是一個以自我為中心的人，凡事只要確認自己問心無愧，你就不會在意別人怎麼說。你相信清者自清，謠言總會有澄清的一天。所以你一點也不擔心那些有心混淆視聽的人。

D：你是個會受謠言影響的人，在短時間內你會處於情緒不穩，且需要療傷的狀態。可是不用多久你就能痊癒。你會發現生活中有其它更重要的事，所以你的注意力會被轉移。而在那之後，就好像那些事情從來沒有發生過一樣。

心理知識補一補

價格協商

　　價格協商（**Price Negotiation**）指的多半是在公司對公司之間的生意價格討論，大的會是以透過會議的方式作協商，而一般常見的則是對話中所見到的請已合作過的業務報價。而在中文裡有一個成語可以很貼切的形容，就是「討價還價」。

　　在對話當中，Steve 跟 Rosemary 兩個人之間上演有如諜對諜的情節，其實很難說哪一方的處理方式不對，兩方都有各自的考量。在心理學研究中指出，巧妙地運用數字在產品價格上，能為公司帶來更多的收益，而這與經濟學理論中所說的 Price Sensitive 相關。例如在對話中 Steve 建議 Rosemary 以更優惠的價格改採購另一種鍵盤，但基於客戶要求，所以可以說是沒有替代品，所以身為賣方的 Steve 則可以考慮不用給相當的折扣，也不需降低最小採購量。而 Rosemary 也利用針對採購量上數字的微幅調整，希望能拿到最優惠的價格。

　　最後 Steve 是以快刀斬亂麻的方式，跟 Rosemary 說清楚他的立場，用報價單的 7 日期限讓對方考慮合作的可能性。在職場中，尤其是從事業務的人員，常會遇到諸如此類的人情壓力。是要在公司規定上讓步，還是公事公辦就要端看個人智慧及公司給你的權限來決定囉，如果真的無法讓步，建議是要以誠懇的態度將情況說清楚，千萬不要扼殺了自己下一次可能會做成生意的機會。

辦公室篇

貿易篇

業務篇

行銷篇

感情篇

Unit 2 我家送到你家

 前情提要

Jason is making a call to Matthew from his factory to discuss on shipping and delivery details.

Jason 從工廠致電給 Matthew 來討論運送細節。

 角色介紹

Jason- The shuffler supplier of Matthew's company（Matthew 公司的洗牌機供應商）

Matthew- The sales representative of shufflers from Jason's company（Jason 公司洗牌機的銷售代表）

Kelly- Matthew's assistant（Matthew 的助理）

 情境對話

Jason: Hi Matthew, I am Jason calling to find out how you would like the 16 shufflers to be shipped, by air or by sea? Will you arrange shipment from your side as it is F.O.B. terms?

嗨，Matthew，我是 Jason 打來問你想要如何運送這 16 台洗牌機，透過空運還是海運？因為是 F.O.B.的條款所以你會從你們那邊安排寄送嗎？

Matthew: Hi, Jason, we would like you to ship them via FedEx using our account

嗨，Jason，我們希望你們用我們的帳戶透過

and please ship them directly to our clients. Kelly, my assistant will email you our invoice to put in and go with the shipment. You said you can deliver them on the 20th, correct?

FedEx 直接運送到我們客戶手上，我的助理 Kelly 會 email 給你我們的發票給你們隨貨放在貨裡面，你說過你 20 號會寄送它們，正確嗎？

Kelly: Matthew, Tsaga group just emailed to rush us to let them get the machines on the 13th, can you check the possibility with Jason, please?

Matthew，Tsaga 集團剛剛 email 來催我們讓他們可以在 13 號就拿到機器，你可以和 Jason 確認一下可能性嗎？

Matthew: Wait Jason, **this order is now urgently in need to be shipped, is there any chance you might be able to deliver them like on the 10th?** This is a big group we are trying to impress them and we hope to make your shuffler of the only choice across their group.

等等，Jason，現在這個訂單急著需要運送，有任何機會讓你可以在大概 10 號就寄送給他們嗎？這是一個我們試圖要使其驚艷的大集團，然後我們也希望你們可以成為他們集團之中洗牌機的唯一選擇。

Jason: Well, if you put it that way, even though this is not what we agreed on, I will see what I can do.

嗯，如果你這樣說的話，即使這不是我們一開始同意好的，我會看看我能做什麼。

Matthew: **Okay, we count on you for the good news.**

好的，我們靠你給好消息了。

Part 2

 前情提要

Matthew is calling from the office to Jason asking about a situation of Jason's delivered goods.

Matthew 從辦公室打去給 Jason 詢問關於他已送達的貨物的狀況。

 角色介紹

Jason: The shuffler supplier of Matthew's company（Matthew 公司的洗牌機供應商）

Matthew: The sales representative of shufflers from Jason's company（Jason 公司洗牌機的銷售代表）

Kelly: Matthew's assistant（Matthew 的助理）

 情境對話

Matthew: Hi, Jason is Matthew, we have a situation here, I just got off a phone call with our client, the one you said to do partial shipments, 8 machines at a time remember?

嗨 Jason，是 Matthew，我們這裡有個狀況，我剛跟我們客戶講完電話，那個你說要分批裝運的，一次 8 台機器的，記得嗎？

Jason: Yes, Matthew I believe they have received the machines on 9th, we had to work extra shifts to speed up on production and testing, I hope they are satisfied.

是的 Matthew，我相信他們在 9 號就有收到機器了，我們是用加班來加速生產還有測試的，我希望他們是滿意的。

Matthew: They are happy about the early arrival that is true, but they are complaining about the quality, more than

他們對於提早到貨是開心的沒錯，但是他們在抱怨品質，一半以上的機器都

half of the machines are defected, and springs are falling out and wires are loosen and buttons are not functioning, etc. **I have to say I am very upset with you.**

損毀了，而且彈簧脫落還有線鬆掉，以及按鈕無法作用，諸如此類的，我不得不說我對你們很失望。

Jason: I am really sorry to hear such bad news, maybe because we were too eager to make this order perfect… Matthew, can you please have them send us pictures of the defective parts, so we can make a record and we will send over new parts for them to replace first thing in the morning.

聽到這樣的壞消息我真的很抱歉，也許是因為我們太求好心切想把這個訂單做的完美。Matthew，你可以請他們傳毀損的零件照片給我們嗎？我們就可以做一個紀錄，然後明天一大早就寄給他們新的零件。

Matthew: Jason, we do not want this to happen again, make sure the next shipment is perfect, please provide us a tracking number of the parts once available.

Jason，我們不希望這種情形再次發生，請確保下一批貨是完美的，等有零件的追蹤號碼的時候請提供給我們。

辦公室心情隨筆

 Jason:

I have to call Matthew to see how to arrange the shipment of the 16 shufflers. They want them to be shipped to the client sooner than what we agreed on, but they are giving a good reason, so I have to see what I can do because we have to give them our support when they need us to. I will have our team to speed up on production and testing and to deliver the goods earlier than they expect.

　　我必須打給 Matthew 看要怎麼安排這 16 台洗牌機。他們想要比起我們同意的更早讓機器送到客戶那，但是他們給了我們一個很好的理由，所以我要看看我能怎麼做，因為當他們需要我們的支持的時候我們要給。我會讓我們的團隊加速生產和測試，然後就可以把貨物比他們期待得更快送達。

Matthew is telling me that they are facing a problem, but the partial goods should have arrived. What? How come most of the machines are not perfect, now I do not know how to face Matthew, and our product's reputation will be affected. I have to ask Matthew to have them send over pictures of the actual defected situation. Luckily, it is just a partial shipment, and we still have another chance to win back their trust. I have to ensure the next shipment will have zero mistakes. I feel so sorry for putting Matthew in this kind of situation.

　　Matthew 現在告訴我說他們面臨到問題了，但是分批的貨物應該已經抵達了。什麼？大部分的機器怎麼會不是完美的，現在我不知道要怎麼面對 Matthew 了，而且我們產品的聲譽會被影響。我必須要求 Matthew 讓他們傳照片來看實際損壞的狀況。幸好，這只是部分的貨物，我們還有另一個贏回他們信任的機會。我必須確保下批貨物是零錯

誤 的 。 置 Matthew 於 這 個 處 境 我 感 到 很 抱 歉 。

 Matthew:

These 16 shufflers are very important to us, so we will choose to ship them at all costs, as long as they are fast and safely delivered to this client.

這 16 台 洗 牌 機 對 我 們 來 說 非 常 重 要 , 所 以 我 們 會 選 擇 不 惜 代 價 運 送 它 們 , 只 要 可 以 夠 快 且 安 全 到 達 這 個 客 戶 那 邊 。

Now Tsaga group is rushing us for this shipment, and we must get them what they want, I want to satisfy them. I will see if Jason can compromise and see if it is even possible for him to speed up on his side. Jason now sounds positive, maybe there is hope.

現 在 Tsaga 集 團 在 催 促 我 們 這 批 貨 了 , 我 們 必 須 給 他 們 他 們 想 要 的 , 我 想 要 滿 足 他 們 。 我 要 看 Jason 能 不 能 妥 協 , 然 後 甚 至 看 是 否 他 那 邊 可 能 可 以 加 速 。 Jason 現 在 聽 起 來 是 肯 定 的 , 也 許 是 有 希 望 的 。

Hope Jason will deliver good news, so we will not let Tsaga group down for our very first transaction.

希 望 Jason 可 以 傳 達 好 消 息 來 , 我 們 會 讓 Tsaga 集 團 在 我 們 這 初 次 的 訂 單 就 失 望 。

Seriously? Tsaga group gave a negative feedback due to too many broken parts on the machines of the first shipment. I must ask Jason to explain himself. We trust him that much, he should not have made this kind of mistake. It seems like they just wanted to get it done soon for us and they did not do it on purpose and also I can tell they feel sorry. All we can do now is to do something about the first shipment and keep an eye on the next shipment now.

Part 2

　　當真？Tsaga group 因為這第一批貨物裡的機器有太多損壞的零件而給我們負面的評價。我必須要求 Jason 給個交代。我們這麼相信他，他不該犯下這樣的錯誤。看來他們只是想快點把這個單做好，並不是故意的，而且我可以看受到他們覺得抱歉。現在我們能做的指是對於首批貨做點什麼以及注意下一批貨物了。

 好好用句型

★ **This order is now urgently in need to be shipped. Is there any chance you might be able to deliver them like on the 10th ?**

現在這個訂單急著需要運送，有任何機會讓你可以在大概 **10** 號就寄送給他們嗎？

urgently in need 急需

　　Or you can say:

- In a great need.

  急需。

- Desperately in need.

  迫切地需要。

★ **Okay we count on you for the good news.**

好的，我們靠你給好消息了。

count on you 依靠你/靠你了

　　Or you can say:

- Lean on you.

  依靠你。

- It's all up to you now.

  現在全靠你了。

★ **I have to say I am very upset with you.**
我不得不說我對你們很失望。

upset with you 對你失望

Or you can say:

- **I'm disappointed in you.**
  對你感到失望。
- **You let me down.**
  你讓我失望。

 心理小測試

危機處理能力

Q 假如有天你打開冰箱，看到一罐紙盒裝的牛奶倒頭就喝，喝了一大口之後進去之後，你才發現已經過期了，此時你第一時間會：

A：停下來不喝，並把喝進去的吐出來

B：不以為意，照喝不誤

C：趕快去看醫生

D：停下來不喝，並把牛奶倒掉

測驗結果
請見下頁

測驗結果

A：你對任何事的處理方式通常是自己做自己的事，不會想太多．
因此你對危機應變能力也較單純，成熟度一般。

B：看似粗枝大葉，但其實你冷靜理性，已經有不少牛奶是可以
長期保存的，至少你知道這點。

C：選擇趕快去看醫生的你，是一個相當神經質而且不太能忍受
壓力的人。 一旦面對危險，常會亂了陣腳，也有過度自我
防禦的現象。

D：不但不敢再喝，還想到防止他人也誤喝，趕快把過期牛奶丟
掉的人，成熟度高，當面臨危險時，也懂得如何去主動照顧
他人。

心理知識補一補

 「急」與「催促」

　　相信有些人跟這個單元中的 Jason 一樣，曾在職場中遇到這一種被「過河拆橋」的情況。明明在合約上寫的交貨日期不是那麼早，但卻因為對方要求，或是提了一些聽起來誘人的條件，所以就答應了。但因為準備時間不充足，出了差錯，受到對方的指責，這時候只能自己默默承受。

　　其實，在對方表示「**急**」，或是有「**催促**」的時候，你就已經不知不覺地進入了對方的圈套。這是一種在談判協商時常會使用的技巧之一，以事情緊急為由，將時間轉換成籌碼。根據一項在 1978 年時所做的心理實驗，以三句不同的問法詢問使用影印機的人：

(1) 不好意思，可以讓我用一下影印機嗎？

(2) 不好意思，可以讓我用一下影印機嗎？因為我在趕時間。

(3) 不好意思，可以讓我用一下影印機嗎？因為我要影印。

　　其中第 2 句有表達出「急」，有 94％ 的人會答應，而第 3 句聽起來也有急的感覺，所以有 93％，而最少的第一句則為 60％。心理學家分析，這是因為人類的同理心，所以在當時的情況往往會失去部分判斷力，而答應對方要求。對話中 Matthew 說的類似金光黨常用的手法，有「千萬不要錯過這一個千載難逢的好機會！」的感覺。

　　所以要記得，下次在遇上職場「金光黨」時，噢不，是夥伴啦！要小心這樣的技巧，在答應之前，一定要先衡量情況是否可行，再做決定！

Unit 3 我是談判王

 前情提要

CTS Company （South Africa） is the main shuffler distributor of GentFul Company （UK）. GentFul recently upgraded their shuffler from version 5 （V5） to version 6 （V6） and GentFul tried to have CTS upgrade all their V5 machines to V6. They are now in the meeting room having some discussions about this.

CTS 公司（南非）是 GentFul 公司洗牌機的主經銷商，GentFul 最近升級了它們的洗牌機，從版本 5 到版本 6。他們現在在會議室裡面進行關於此事的討論。

 角色介紹

Johnny Whiskin: The executive director of CTS Company（CTS 公司的執行董事）

Teddy West: The general manager of GentFul Company（GentFul 公司的總經理）

 情境對話

Teddy West: Johnny, have you seen the exchange plan that I email you?

Johnny，你有看了我 email 給你的交換計畫了嗎？

Johnny Whiskin: Yes, they look good.

有啊，看起來很好。但是

However, we have a problem with the upgrading cost from V5 to V6.

對於 V5 升級到 V6 的花費我們有點問題。

Teddy West: We called it the conversion cost and it is the lowest already.

我們稱它為轉換費用,而且已經是最低價了。

Johnny Whiskin: **I understand you have your own expenses, but let me just remind you that since V5 failed, clients now have no faith in our machines.** They are not willing to pay this.

我明白你們有自己的開銷,但是讓我提醒你,因為 V5 失敗了,現在客戶對我們的機器沒有信心。他們不願意付這個錢。

Teddy West: Johnny, we did not make all the works for free and to consider the production cost… this really cannot get any lower.

我們做所有工作都不是免費的,而且考慮到成本……,這真的不能再更低了。

Johnny Whiskin: Teddy, we are after a free of charge on the upgrades. Listen, when V5 was launched, CTS Africa supported GentFul more than any other distributors and we sold many machines, but then clients asked for refunds which were over USD300,000, also when the machine was in patent infringement, we got law suits, and we did not ask GentFul to bear any.

Teddy,我們想要的是免費升等。聽著,當 V5 推出的時候,CTS 南非比起其他經銷商是更支持 GentFul 的,也賣了很多機器,但是後來客戶要求退錢,我們退了超過 USD300,000,還有當機器有專利侵權時,我們也吃了很多官司,而我們都沒有讓 GentFul 承擔。

辦公室篇

貿易篇

業務篇

行銷篇

感情篇

Part 2

Teddy West: Okay, that is quite convincing, and I feel for you, but if this time V6 works, you'd better bring us lots of sales.

好的，那是蠻有說服力的而且我對你深表同情，但是如果這次 V6 成功了，你最好帶給我們很多銷售量。

Johnny Whiskin: Of course.

當然。

 前情提要

Marcus is in the office asking Johnny about tips of negotiation.

Marcus 在辦公室問 Johnny 關於談判的技巧。

 角色介紹

Johnny- The executive director of CTS Company（CTS 公司的業務推廣經理）

Marcus- The business development manager of CTS Company（CTS 公司的執行董事）

 情境對話

Marcus: A little bird told me you made the GentFul exchange plan free, good on you Johnny! I have tried for several times, but they just ignored my request.

我聽說你讓 GentFul 的交換計劃變免費了，Johnny 你好樣的！我嘗試了好幾次了但他們都忽視我的請求。

Johnny: **You just did not get the hang of it I guess.** Learn from me young man!

我猜你只是沒掌握到其中的訣竅。年輕人跟我學著點！

Marcus: I am all ears! Tell me! What exactly did you do or say to them?

我洗耳恭聽！告訴我！你到底對他們做了還是說了什麼？

Johnny: Well, I sort of left them no choice, I played the pity card.

這個嘛，我有點沒給他們留下選擇的餘地，我用了裝可憐這招。

Marcus: You played the pity card? How?

你用裝可憐的招？怎麼用的？

Johnny: Just all that we paid a lot of money and the customer lost faith in us, and I told them it is time for them to support us back, something like that. **I just wanted to get them step into our shoes; thus, I had to awake their empathy and sympathy.** Simple as that!

就是那些我們付了很多錢還讓客戶失去信心，然後我告訴他們是時候該他們支持我們回來了，諸如此類的。我只是想讓他們設身處地為我們想，因此我不得不喚醒他們的同理心還有同情心。就這麼簡單！

Marcus: It's easy for you to say because you are so good at negotiating and you can be very convincing when you try to get something, but you taught me a lesson, indeed.

你說的很容易，因為你很善於談判，而且當你試圖得到什麼的時候你就非常有說服力，但你的確給我上了一堂課。

辦公室心情隨筆

Teddy:

I need to chase up with Johnny about that exchange plan because we really need to get this done soon.

> 我需要追一下 Johnny 關於交換計劃的事，因為我們真的需要快把這個處理好。

Johnny is not okay with the conversion cost we quoted, but there is no way we are giving them free for the exchange. However, I will listen to him first. He definitely comes prepared, but he still needs to convince me.

> Johnny 對於我們報的轉換費用覺得不行，但是我們不可能給他們免費交換。但是我還是會先聽聽他怎麼說，他應該是有備而來的，但是他還是需要說服我。

Johnny is giving that speech again, and he has been using those lines for a while now, but yes we did have more support from them than any others, if it wasn't for them, there wouldn't be V6 now. I do feel grateful and we do owe them that much for having them to pay all the refunds and law suit charges. I am buying this story for the one last time because we really need to move on to the next generation. If we have to have full focus on the new machine, we need to have the last few machines upgraded. Johnny gives persuasive speeches all the time, and he is so good at this. Okay, in order to get his continuous support for the next generation, we will give him what he wants.

> Johnny 又在講那套了，且他用這些台詞已經好一陣子了，但是沒錯，比起其他人他們真的比較支持我們，如果不是他們，也不會有現在的 V6。我真的感激也覺得讓他們付所有退款還有訴訟費是真的欠他們

那們多。我要最後一次被這個說法說服了，因為我們需要前進到下一代，如果我們要一心專注在新機器上，我們就需要把最後幾台機器升級。Johnny 總是能做很有說服力的談話，而且他真的很會這個。好吧，為了繼續得到他們對下一代的支持，我們就給他他想要的吧。

Johnny:

I was surprised that Teddy dares to ask money from us for the upgrades. After what they have put us through, there is no way that we are going to pay any cents for this. Let me just simply remind him how much we have paid and lost because of them, they should once again being thoughtful and understand us. All I am asking is not to charge us for the exchange, so we can quickly upgrade all the failing machines and end this mess. If this new generation really works and performs much better than the previous one, we can easily sell them and earn money for both of us.

Teddy 有膽跟我們要升級的錢我感到訝異。在他們讓我們經歷的之後，我們不可能要付這筆錢的。讓我簡單再次提醒他我們為了他們付了多少錢和失去多少，他們應該會再次體諒跟理解。我所要求的只是不要收我們交換的錢，然後就可以快點把所有失敗的機器升級，然後結束這亂子。如果這新一代的真的成功而且表現比上一代好很多，我們很輕易可以賣出，為雙方賺錢。

Okay, it is finally a done deal. Marcus wants to know my negotiations tips. I, of course, can share this with him, but it is easier to say than done. If he's got experiences like me..., but he is not. Skill comes with experiences. Maybe in a couple of years he can. Anyway, I still appreciate Teddy for making things easy.

好了，談成了。Marcus 想知道我協商的秘訣，我當然可以跟他分享，但是說起來容易做起來難。如果他有我的經驗……，但他沒有。經驗越多，技巧越熟練。也許再幾年他就可以吧。總之，我還是很感激 Teddy 讓事情變的好辦。

好好用句型

★ **I understand you have your own expenses, but let me just remind you that since V5 failed, clients now have no faith in our machines.**

我明白你們有自己的開銷，但是讓我提醒你，因為 **V5** 失敗了，現在客戶對我們的機器沒有信心。

no faith in…對……沒有信心 / lose faith in…對……失去信心

Or you can say:

- Lose credit / Lose credibility.
  失去信用。／失去可信度。
- Lose confidence.
  失去自信心。

★ **You just did not get the hang of it I guess.**

我猜你只是沒掌握到其中的訣竅。

get the hang of it 掌握訣竅

Or you can say:

- Get the tips.
  得到訣竅/技巧。
- Learned the ropes.
  掌握訣竅。（大多用於工作上）

★ **I just wanted to get them step into our shoes; thus, I had to**

辦公室篇

貿易篇

業務篇

行銷篇

感情篇

awake their empathy and sympathy.

我只是想讓他們設身處地為我們想，因此我不得不喚醒他們的同理心還有同情心。

Step into our shoes.

設身處地為我們著想。

Or you can say:

● Have our best interests at heart.

　處處為我們的利益著想。

● Put yourself in our place. / Put yourself in our position.

　設身處地為我們想。

 心理小測試

職場成就滿意度

Q 假如有一把鑰匙掉落在水池附近，當你在尋找它時，請運用個人的想像力與直覺，請問你認為它會是用下列哪一種材料製成的？

A：鐵

B：木

C：金

D：銀

E：銅

測驗結果
請見下頁

測 驗 結 果

A：你是一個非常了解現實的人，你很少做無謂的空想，用常人的思維方式思考和處理問題，與周遭的人相處和諧，不惹事生非。但現在的你可能正處於人生低潮。

B：你的內心深處似乎暗藏著對現實生活的不滿，或是覺得非常疲倦。感覺做什麼事都麻煩，缺乏嘗試新事物的動力，現在的你渴望依附在強人的身上。

C：你現在的事業非常旺。在你周遭充滿了機會，可以實現你的理想或夢想，而且新事物也會不斷帶給你好運。

D：你是個懂得運用智慧找出合理解決方案的人。你面臨問題只要仔細思考後，便能做出反應。你在接受別人給的意見時態度非常謹慎。你的財運很強盛，有致富的可能性。

E：你很有自信也有能力，可以俐落處理事情。但當面臨討厭的事物時，你誰的話也聽不進去，認為自己是最重要的。你似乎可以兼顧得很好。現在正是你放手一搏的好時機。

心理知識補一補

◈ 職場上的談判之道

在職場上，一定不可避免地有會需要協商的時候，而這個時候，要如何「**談判**」，則是每個上班族都必修的人際關係課。一般來說，只要是拿出誠懇的態度，將事情說清楚講明白，大多可以得到對方的支持。

但在這一段對話中，Johnny 有提到他用了「裝可憐」這一招，也就是我們說的「哀兵政策」。哀兵政策是從老子第六十九章的「哀兵勝矣」延伸出來的。本意是說受到欺侮的士兵因此生出勇氣對抗敵人。但現在則被解釋成裝可憐，讓對方輕敵。

但事實上，Johnny 的成功並不盡是來自於哀兵政策的成功。因為在 Teddy 的心情隨筆中，他知道 Johnny 又要來那一套了。但是基於雙方對於這一個項目的發展都還抱著期待，以及 Johnny 也有提出關於之前侵權官司的部分，所以這一次的協商才能成功落幕。由此可知將事實釐清，以及釋出適當的善意，才是能達到雙贏局面（Win-Win Situation）的最佳途徑。

辦公室篇

貿易篇

業務篇

行銷篇

感情篇

Unit 4 客訴麥擱卡

 前情提要

Claire is calling to BS Shoe Shop's customer service department to make a complaint about their sales.

Claire 打去 BS 鞋店的客服部投訴他們一個銷售員。

 角色介紹

Claire- A customer of the BS Shoe Shop（一個 BS 鞋店的客人）

Phoebe- A sales from the BS Shoe Shop（一個 BS 鞋店的銷售員）

Louis- Works in the customer service department of BS Shoe Shop（在 BS 鞋店的客服部門工作）

 情境對話

Louis: Hello, this is Louis. How can I help you today?

您好，我是 Louis，今天有什麼可以幫到您的嗎？

Claire: I visited BS Shoe Shop two days ago, and I was not very happy about one of your sales there. She kept using her phone while I was trying to ask her to get my sizes for shoes. **She gave me an attitude when I called her for her service.** There is more, she said my feet

我兩天前去了 BS 鞋，我對你們那邊的一個銷售員不太滿意。她在我叫她幫我拿尺寸的時候一直用手機。我叫她服務的時候還口氣很差。還有，她說我的腳胖穿你們的鞋不好

are too fat to look good in your shoes. That was very impolite.

看。這是非常不禮貌的。

Louis: Oh no, how terrible! May I first of all have your name, please? **Also, do you have the name of the sales, because we take this kind of thing very seriously.**

噢不,這太糟糕了啊!我可以先問您怎麼稱呼嗎?另外,您有沒有那個銷售員的名字,因為我們對於這種事情是很嚴肅看待的。

Claire: Sure I did, I purposely wrote down her name. Her name is Phoebe and my name is Claire, Claire Huang.

我當然有,我有特別寫下她名字。她的名字是Phoebe,我的名字是Claire,Claire 黃。

Louis: Claire, I apologize for our poor service and your awful experience. Bad attitude is not allowed in the BS Shoe Shop and mobile phones are absolutely prohibited during work. Claire, we are sorry for what happened, and I will report her up and they will take actions immediately. Can we call you back tomorrow at this number?

Claire,我為我們服務品質差以及您可怕的經歷道歉,態度不好在 BS 鞋店是不允許的,手機在上班時間也是被禁止的。Claire,對於所發生的事我們感到抱歉,我會上報她,然後他們應該馬上會採取行動。明天我們可以打這個號碼給您嗎?

Claire: Yes.

可以。

Louis: Thank you. Bye.

謝謝您,再見。

辦公室篇

貿易篇

業務篇

行銷篇

感情篇

Part 2

 前情提要

Louis is calling Claire on the behalf of BS Shoe Shop about her complaint.

Louis 代表 BS 鞋店打給 Claire 關於她的投訴。

 角色介紹

Claire- A customer of the BS Shoe Shop（一個 BS 鞋店的客人）
Phoebe- A sales from the BS Shoe Shop（一個 BS 鞋店的銷售員）
Louis- Works in the customer service department of BS Shoe Shop
（在 BS 鞋店的客服部門工作）

 情境對話

Louis: Hello Claire, this is Louis from BS Shoe Shop, we talked on the phone yesterday regarding our sales named Phoebe.

Claire 您好，我是 BS 鞋店的 Louis，我們昨天有講電話，關於我們一個叫 Phoebe 的銷售員。

Claire: Yes.

是的。

Louis: I am calling to inform you that our company fired Phoebe yesterday, she will no longer work for us.

我是打來告知您，Phoebe 昨天被我們公司解雇了，她將不再為我們工作。

Claire: Oh… I was not after that. I just wanted her to get a warning. Are you saying that she lost her job due to my complaint yesterday?

噢……我本來要的不是這樣的，我只是想要她得到個警告。你是說她被解雇是因為我昨天的投訴嗎？

Louis: We have got many of complaints about Phoebe, it was not her first time, and we have given her chances. She lost her job on her, not because of you Claire.

我們有接到很多關於 Phoebe 的投訴了，那並不是她第一次了，我們也給了她機會了，她自己讓她失去了工作，並不是因為您 Claire。

Claire, as a compensation, we will give you all the shoes you have tried on the other day for free and we will put you into our VIP database; therefore, you will have discounts for every future purchases. Are you okay with this arrangement, Claire?

Claire，作為補償，我們會免費送您那天試過的所有鞋，以及我們會把您放入我們的 VIP 資料庫，因此，您以後消費就會有折扣。Claire，對於這個安排，您覺得可以嗎？

Claire: **Wow! I did not see that coming!** It is very nice of you! I am totally okay with it.

哇！我沒料到！你們真好！我完全 ok。

Louis: Good to know, I will put you on hold and transfer to other department for details. Have a great evening and BS Shoe Shop welcome your call anytime.

太好了，細節的話，我會把您保留然後轉給其他部門。祝您有個美好的夜晚，BS 鞋店隨時歡迎您來電。

辦公室心情隨筆

 Claire:

I must make a complaint about that terrible staff from BS Shoe Shop, they should not hire such an unprofessional employee at all. If she does not know how to serve and respect people, how can she stand in the service industry? What a shame on her.

我必須投訴一下那個 BS Shop 的職員，他們根本不該雇用如此不專業的員工。如果她不知道怎麼服務或者尊重人，她如何可以在服務業站得住腳。真是為她感到丟臉。

This Louis is very kind and polite, I hope he can truly report that staff up and get some punishment. Making this phone call is so right, now I feel better.

這個 Louis 真和善和有禮貌，我希望他真的可以上報這個員工並給她懲罰。打這通電話真是對極了，現在我覺得好多了。

What? I got that staff fired? I did not want her to lose her job though. Okay, looks like it is not entirely my fault since she already has records. Wow, they are giving me more than I expected! All the shoes I tried that day are plenty. I no longer need to purchase any shoes for years, I think. Putting me into their VIP database is also super generous because they usually require a lot of purchases in order to be one of the VIPs. BS Shoe Shop really cares what we think and our opinions and our feelings actually mean something to them.

什麼？我讓這個員工被炒了？我並沒有想要讓她失去工作。好吧，看來這不完全是我的錯，因為她已經有記錄了。哇，他們要給我的超出我期望的好多！所有那些我那天試過的鞋有好多，我想我好多年不需要買鞋子了。把我放在他們 VIP 資料庫也是超級大方，因為他們通常要求好多次購買才能成為 VIP。BS Shoe Shop 真的在乎我們的想法以及意見，還有我們的感受真的對他們而言是重要的。

 Louis:

Here comes another complaint, hope this is not something that is really nothing. I prefer to deal with a real issue and assist those really in need. It is tiring for getting calls for ridiculous complaints, and even people call in for chatting.

另一個抱怨又要來了，希望這不是根本沒什麼的事情。我比較喜歡處理真正的事情還有協助真的需要幫忙的。接聽到荒唐的抱怨真的很累人，甚至還有些人是打來聊天的。

This customer is poor, do BS really have an employee acts that way and treats customers like that? This staff embarrasses us, I have to report her and let that staff know how wrong she is. I have to apologize for her unacceptable and absurd behaviors to this customer. I need to let this customer know and feel how sorry we are and how much we value this kind of matter.

這位客人好可憐，BS 真的有員工這樣做還那樣對客人的嗎？這個職員真丟我們的臉，我必須上報她然後讓這個職員知道她做的有多錯。我必須替她不可接受和荒唐的行為致歉。我必須讓這位客人知道且感受到我們有多抱歉，以及我們如何重視這種事情。

Okay, now I am calling the poor customer back and let her know what sort of actions we have taken and will take. I hope she will be satisfied and will still be willing to visit our shops in the future.

好的，現在我要回電話給這可憐的客人，然後讓她知道我們做了什麼動作以及會做什麼。我希望她會滿意而且以後會仍然願意光顧我們的店。

辦公室篇

貿易篇

業務篇

行銷篇

感情篇

Part 2

Good, she likes it all, I am glad we keep one customer and I assume she in the future might be our loyal customer.

很好，她都喜歡，我很高興我們留住這位客人，而且我認為她以後會變成我們的忠實客戶。

🔧 好好用句型

★ **She gave me an attitude when I called her for her service.**

我叫她服務的時候還口氣很差。

give an attitude 口氣不好／口氣差

Or you can say:

- speak daggers to sb.

  對誰講話很衝／惡意中傷

- vent one's rage on sb.

  對誰發洩怒氣

★ **Also, do you have the name of the sales, because we take this kind of thing very seriously.**

另外，您有沒有那個銷售員的名字，因為我們對於這種事情是很嚴重看待的。

Take it seriously.

認真看待。／ 嚴重看待。（**Take it serious.** 為口語常聽到的，但在文法上並不正確。）

Or you can say:

- We will get down to it.

  我們會開始處理。（含有認真對待、處理之意）

- We don't regard it as trifling matter.

  我們不會將這視為小事。（即含有會認真對待之意）

★ **Wow! I did not see that coming!**

哇！我沒料到！

I did not see that coming.

我沒想到。／我沒料到。

Or you can say:

- I did not expect that.（我沒料想到）
- out of the blue.（出乎意料）

心理小測試

工作效率

Q 假如你是一家新成立的公司的主管，在你剛上任這天的會議上，你希望提出一些方法來解決工作上煩惱的問題，你首先會怎麼做？

A：擬出一個議事日程，充分利用和大家一起討論的時間

B：先給同事彼此之間一定的時間相互了解一下

C：直接讓每個人說出如何解決問題的想法

D：鼓勵每一個人說出他當下腦海裡的任何想法，不管多瘋狂都可以

辦公室篇

貿易篇

業務篇

行銷篇

感情篇

測驗結果

A：你一旦決定了什麼，就會不顧實際困難的去做。雖然勇氣可嘉，但處理小事情可能還可以，當面對大問題時，可能你會因為缺乏溝通而喪失效率。

B：你認為，當一個團體的成員之間關係融洽，每一個人都感到心情舒暢時，你們團隊的工作效率才會高。而在這種情況下，人們才能做出最高貢獻。

C：你的民主作風是不錯，但是太過民主的做法本身卻是有違效率的。

D：你對於每種工作都追求嘗新，但是在新鮮的變化過程中，卻又可能因為缺乏連續性而在執行任務的過程中出現問題。你的工作效率也會因此受到影響。

心理知識補一補

同理心 Empathy

同理心（**Empathy**），也常見被縮寫成 EMP。也稱為是「換位思考」，指得是站在對方的角度及思考方向上，去客觀地，不帶主觀意見地去理解當事人，也可以說是為對方設身處地思考的方式。

在英文裡，有一種蠻恰當的說法可以來形容同理心，那就是 "In someone's shoes."（穿某人的鞋。）因為人的腳丫子有的大、有的小，有的窄、有的寬，有胖有瘦，甚至多多少少左右腳都不太一樣大。所以鞋子大多是要本人穿了才知道合不合適，舒不舒服。也可以說 "Put oneself in someone's shoes."，將自己放到對方的位置上去思考，也就是同理心。

在對話當中，客服 Louis 因為將顧客反應的問題，如感同身受一般地迅速處理，並在處理之後，詳細地與顧客回覆處理情況及 BS Shop 所提供的賠償。雖然在現實生活中可能無法提供客戶這麼多的補償（compensation），但若能在第一時間對抱怨的顧客展現出同理心的話，往往能將顧客的憤怒瞬間降到某種程度，對於之後的相關處理也會省去不少的麻煩。

辦公室篇

貿易篇

業務篇

行銷篇

感情篇

Unit 5 客戶來訪

 前情提要

Wakaba is calling Elise for a visit to her company.

Wakaba 打給 Elise 為了要拜訪她的公司。

 角色介紹

Elise- A sales manager（一位銷售經理）

Wakaba- A client of Elise（一位 Elise 的客戶）

 情境對話

 前情提要

Wakaba: Hi Elise, this is Wakaba, I visited your booth at the G3 exhibition.

嗨 Elise，我是 Wakaba，我在 G3 展覽有到訪妳們的攤位。

Elise: Yes, Wakaba I remember you. How are you? Are you back to Japan?

是啊，Wakaba 我記得妳。妳好嗎？妳回日本了嗎？

Wakaba: Yes, I am in Japan now. **Safe and sound.**

I am calling to chase up on your

對啊，我在日本了。安然無恙。

我打來追一下妳們新的

production progress of your new SD cards. I got the sample back to our company and they have approved to use this within our new line of a digital camera.

SD 卡的生產進度。我把樣品拿回公司，然後他們已經批准使用在我們新的數位相機生產線了。

Elise: Cool! **I have good news in return**, that SD card is finishing soon, they will be out by the end of the month.

酷！那我也回報妳一個好消息，那個 SD 卡塊做完了，它們這個月底前就會出來了。

Wakaba: Good to know! However, can I possibly visit your company to make this order? I was told to check the quality in person, no offense, we just have to make sure it can really fit in our digital camera and if it matches all the requirements.

很高興知道！不過我能夠拜訪你們公司拿這個訂單？我被告知說要親自檢查品質，別介意，我們只是需要確保它是否真的可以裝入我們的數位相機，還有是否真的符合所有要求。

Elise: Absolutely! Though I will be out of the country in 2 weeks and I will be away for 2 months, how soon can you organize this visit may I ask?

當然可以！但是我再兩個禮拜要出國而且會離開 2 個月，我能問妳最快可以安排什麼時候來拜訪嗎？

Wakaba: Next week works for me, I will see you then?

下禮拜我可以，我就到時候見妳囉？

Elise: Okay! I look forward to it.

好的！我期待著。

辦公室篇

貿易篇

業務篇

行銷篇

感情篇

Part 2

 前情提要

Wakaba came to visit Elise's company but Elise was late for their appointment.

Wakaba 來拜訪 Elise 的公司，但是 Elise 卻在約好的時間上遲到了。

 角色介紹

Elise- A sales manager（一位銷售經理）

Wakaba- A client of Elise（一位 Elise 的客戶）

Angela- A receptionist of Elise's company（一位 Elise 公司的接待員）

 情境對話

Wakaba: Hi, I have a 3pm appointment with Elise today.

您好，我今天下午 3 點有和 Elise 預約。

Angela: Yes, Miss Wakaba, please take a seat over there first. I will get her for you.

是的，Wakaba 小姐，請在那邊先坐一下。我會幫妳叫她。

Wakaba: Thank you.

謝謝。

Angela: Sorry but Elise is not in right now, she just finished lunch with a client, she will still need around 10 minutes to be here.

抱歉，但是 Elise 現在不在辦公室裡，她剛和一個客戶吃完午餐，她還需要大概 10 分鐘才能到這裡。

Wakaba: I thought she knew I was coming because I called her to confirm last night.

我以為她知道我要來，因為我昨天晚上有打電話確認。

Angela: Miss Wakaba I am very sorry, I am sure she did not mean to be late.

Wakaba 小姐我非常抱歉，我相信她不是故意遲到的。

Wakaba: I reminded her to be punctual. I hope she has a good reason.

我有提醒她要準時。我希望她有個很好的理由。

Elise: Hi, Wakaba, I am so sorry. **I had to close a deal with a client and it took me more time than I expected.** I would rearrange this lunch meeting with this client if only I could. I hope you understand.

嗨 Wakaba，我很抱歉。我不得不達成一個交易，然後這比我想像中花的時間還久。如果我能重安排跟這個客戶的午餐會議的話，我是會的。我希望妳明白。

Wakaba: It is alright, at least you are here now.

沒關係，至少妳現在在這裡了。

Elise: Thank you for being thoughtful Wakaba, now let us talk inside!

謝謝妳的體諒 Wakaba，現在讓我們去裡面談吧！

辦公室心情隨筆

Wakaba:

The sample I took from Taiwan is now approved for our new digital camera line. Both of the product and that company are reliable. Let me call Elise from that Taiwan company to tell her our intention. Also, I need to find out whether that product is mature enough for our use. I am assigned to visit their company to check on the quality and all that personally.

這個我從台灣拿的樣本，現在被批准給我們新的數位相機生產線了。這個產品和那個台灣的公司都是可靠的。我來打給那家台灣公司的 Elise 告訴她我們的意向，還有我也需要找出是否那個產品對於我們使用上是成熟的。我被指派去拜訪他們公司，去親自查看品質那些的。

It is good that their product is almost available, so that when I visit, I can bring our order back directly.

他們的產品快好了真好，這樣我去拜訪的時候就可以直接把我們的訂單帶回來。

She is saying Elise is not in the office. This is bad. I do not really like people who miss their appointments or be late. Punctuality is like a simple way to show courtesy and respect for others. From what I recall, Elise is very polite. I am certain that she is not like that, she would be on time if she could. However, I did remind her about me coming at this time. Anyway, I will wait for her and hear what she says. Okay, it is not her fault as it is out of her control, I can understand her.

她說 Elise 不在辦公室，真不好。我沒有很喜歡會錯過約會或者遲到的人。守時是對其他人的禮貌及尊重。我印象中，Elise 是很有禮貌的。確定她不是那樣的人，她如果能準時的話會準時的。但是我是有提醒她我會在這個時間來的。總之，我會等她看她怎麼說。好，這不是她的錯因為不是她能控制的，我可以理解她。

 Elise:

Wakaba they really come back to us and they have chosen our product for their company. This is a huge opportunity. I must let her feel how excited we are to be able to work with them when she visits. Our SD card is right on time for making to be a part of their product line. Moreover, she is able to come here while I am in the country. How blessed we are!

Wakaba 他們真的回來找我們了，而且他們選擇了我們給他們公司。這是個很大的機會。等她來的時候，我一定要讓她知道我們有多激動我們能跟他們合作。我們的 SD 卡剛好趕上了可以變成在它們部分生產線裡。還有，她能在我在國內的時候來拜訪。我們真幸運！

Oh no! It looks like this meeting is going to last longer than I thought. I cannot leave right now, but I also surely cannot be late for the appointment with Wakaba. I should close the deal soon. I do not want to keep Wakaba waiting for too long.

噢不！看來這個會議會比我以為的還久，我現在不能離開但是我與 Wakaba 的約也不能遲到。我該快做成這交易，我不想讓 Wakaba 等太久。

Angela called to rush me. I got to be hurry because she said Wakaba is unhappy now.

Angela 打來催我了，我必須快點因為她說 Wakaba 現在不高興了。

Glad that Wakaba can forgive me for being late; otherwise, I will lose this chance for taking through all the details and possibilities with her. I am ready to amaze her.

好險 Wakaba 可以原諒我遲到，否則我就會失去這個可以跟她講所有細節還有可能性的機會。我準備好讓她驚豔了。

Part 2

 好好用句型

★ **Safe and sound.**

安然無恙。（通常指人）

> Or you can say:
>
> ● Safe and quiet.
>   安全無虞。（通常指環境）
> ● In fine feather.
>   精神飽滿。

★ **Cool! I have good news in return.**

酷！那我也回報妳一個好消息

in return 回報

> Or you can say:
>
> ● pay off
>   回報（通常指付出後得到的回報）
> ● be rewarded
>   回報（有種被獎賞之意）

★ **I had to close a deal with a client and it spent me more time they I expected.**

我不得不達成一個交易，然後它比我想像中花的時間還久。

close a deal 達成一個交易／生意成交

> Or you can say:
>
> ● to conclude a deal
>   達成協議
> ● make a deal / have a deal
>   達成交易

心理小測試

談判力

Q 假如有天你突然被一個賣減肥產品的直銷員纏上了，他一直強烈地想要說服你跟他買減肥藥，還直說你太胖必須減肥，此時你會怎麼做呢？

A：很心動，心中盤算著要怎麼跟他殺價

B：覺得很尷尬，而且堅持不買

C：無可奈何的聽他說完，但是沒有要買的意思

D：為了脫身馬上掏錢直接買了

測驗結果
請見下頁

測驗結果

A：你總是會在談判桌上給自己和對方都留有餘地，所以在合作上也給予較大的商量空間。不會拒人於千里，處事也有原則，也會謹慎的考慮利弊。

B：你是個有著絕對原則的人，只要你界定了一條底線，就幾乎沒有任何人可以改變你的想法和決定。你喜歡在談判桌上扮演主導者，一旦對方的看法和妳不同，你會毫不留情的不給面子。

C：你是個好好先生型的人，你做事沒有原則，或者你總是害怕傷到對方，所以你總是在壓抑自己真實的想法。但是合作歸合作，如果濫用好心又毫無原則，是很容易吃虧的。

D：你是個重感情也缺少理性的人，你很衝動，在生活中是個消費狂人，在談判桌上更是腦筋不清楚，常常打腫臉充胖子的答應對方的要求，很容易一下子就會沒了籌碼。

心理知識補一補

守時

在許多寫給職場新鮮人的文章當中，不斷的提到守時的重要性。其實守時的概念也是我們從小到大都一直被灌輸的。

然而這個在職場上被稱為是「軟實力」之一的守時觀念，根據部分心理學家的研究認為這極有可能是天生的。但也有學者認為是後天學得的。以下介紹守時的人有那一些共通的特性。

1. 自控力強：守時的人對於事情很少拖延，跟習慣性遲到的人相較，自我的掌控能力較佳。
2. 多為 A 型性格者：這裡的 A 型指的不是血型，而是 A 型與 B 型人格的分類。A 型人格的特徵有勤奮、追求完美等，所以守時對於他們而言是在人際交往上不可或缺的重要因素。
3. 有責任心：在研究中指出守時的人會比常遲到的人有更重的責任心。
4. 做事謹慎：守時的人為了要能夠準時赴約，總是會為自己預留緩衝的時間，這樣的態度也往往會反映在做其他的事情上。

辦公室篇

貿易篇

業務篇

行銷篇

感情篇

Unit 6 年終尾牙

 前情提要

Stefanie is notifying Margaret and Jung that they are in charge for the annual banquet planning of their company this year.

Stefanie 在告知 Margaret 和 Jung 她們負責今年公司的尾牙籌劃。

 角色介紹

Stefanie- The supervisor of Margaret and Jung（Margaret 和 Jung 的監事）

Margaret- Staff 1（職員 1）

Jung- Staff 2（職員 2）

 情境對話

Stefanie: Margaret and Jung, please come here. **As you know that our company draws for who is in charge of the annual banquet every year,** this year they drew out you two.

Margaret 還有 Jung，請過來這裡。如妳們所知，我們公司每年是以抽籤的方式決定誰負責尾牙。今年抽到妳們兩個。

Margaret: What? I have never planned such thing!

什麼？我沒有計畫過這樣的事！

Jung: Good! This year we can finally have

很好！今年我們終於可以

some real fun. **Do we get to decide all the details?** Themes and food and all?

有一些真正的樂趣。難道我們能夠決定所有細節嗎？主題和食物還有所有的？

Stefanie: Margaret, it's not that difficult. I will send you some proposal examples. Learn from others and make changes.

Margaret，那沒那麼難，我會寄給妳一些企畫書的例子。向別人學習然後做點改變。

Yes, Jung. You decide what we eat and what we wear and all those. As long as you do not got them over the budget.

對啊，Jung，由妳們來決定我們要吃什麼還有穿什麼還有一些有的沒的。只要妳們不讓它們超出預算。

Jung: Margaret, it should be fine. **We can work this out together**, believe me, I am like a natural party planner and think about what you wish to set for prizes.

Margaret 應該沒事啦，我們可以一起想辦法，相信我，我就像是一個天生的派對規劃人，而且妳可以想想妳想要設定什麼獎項。

Margaret: I just hate planning and just want to have fun.

我只是討厭規劃然後只是想要玩。

Jung: I already have plenty of ideas in my mind. Let us meet for discussion this weekend, okay? You still got 5 days to

我腦海裡已經有好多想法了，這週末我們來見面討論這件事好嗎？妳還有 5

think. Before the end of the day, I will give you a task allocation list, so you know what to focus.

Margret: That is great!

天可以想。在今天結束之前我會給妳一個工作分配表，這樣妳就知道妳要專注在什麼上面了。

那太好了！

 前情提要

Margaret and Jung are meeting in a coffee shop for the planning of their company's annual banquet this year.

Margaret 和 Jung 在咖啡店為了她們負責公司今年尾牙的籌劃而碰面。

 角色介紹

Margaret- Staff 1（職員１）
Jung- Staff 2（職員２）

 情境對話

Jung: Margaret, have you picked the place and dress code for our annual banquet yet?

Margaret 你有選好今年尾牙的場地還有服裝規定了嗎？

Margaret: I thought we can hold one like usual; we just choose a restaurant that can accommodate 500 people and wear whatever.

我想說我們如以往那樣辦，我們就選個可以容納 500 人的餐廳，然後隨便穿。

Margaret: Or do you have any other suggestions?

或者妳有任何其它建議嗎？

Jung: Well, we can book a hotel ballroom

這個嘛，我們可以預約飯

and ask them to cater food, as for the dress code, each table should have a color theme thus everyone sitting in the same table should wear the same color.

店的交誼廳然後請他們準備食物，至於服裝規定，每一桌應該要有個顏色的主題，因此每個坐在同一桌的人應該穿一樣的顏色。

Margaret: That sounds really fun and creative. We will do that. Okay, now you got me thinking. I just have another idea that pops out. You know, every year each department sits with people from their own department right? How about this year, before the annual banquet, everyone draw lots to decide their table? They can then find out what color to wear, too. However, more importantly, people can get to know people from other departments and make some new friends.

那聽起來好好玩也好有創意。我們就這麼做。好，現在妳讓我開始想了。我正有另一個想法跑出來。你知道，每年每個部門都和他們自己同部門的坐，對吧？不如今年，在尾牙之前，大家抽籤來決定自己坐哪桌？他們就也可以知道自己要穿什麼顏色。然而最重要的是，人們可以有機會認識來自其他部門的人，然後交些新朋友。

Jung: That is so cool! For prizes we put all Apple products on the list, the higher the price, the bigger the prize would be.

這太酷了！有關獎項的話，我們就把所有 Apple 的產品放上清單，越高價位的就越大獎。

Margaret: Well done! Glad that we are on the same page.

做得好！我們有一樣的想法真好。

辦公室篇

貿易篇

業務篇

行銷篇

感情篇

Part 2

辦公室心情隨筆

Margaret:

Why me! I hate organizing and planning things! I am a girl and girls just want to have fun! I just want to have fun! Okay, we can just make some minor changes from last year and everyone would think it is different.

為什麼是我！我討厭組織和計劃事情！我是女生，女生只想要玩樂啊！我只想要玩！好，我們可以就從去年的做些微改變，然後大家就會以為這是不一樣的。

Jung looks so excited, and she is going to assign tasks for me, and hope I do not have to decide too much.

Jung 看起來好興奮，然後她要分配任務給我，希望我不用決定太多。

Okay, now we can talk about the annual banquet planning. I do not have any fresh ideas. Hope she can live with it.

好，現在我們要來討論尾牙籌備了，我沒有任何新鮮的想法，希望她能接受。

Her suggestions are awesome! Yes, we should make some fun changes! This is getting more and more interesting! She now makes me see the good side of being in charge for this event. If we have a say, then I want to sit with colleagues from other departments, and I want to meet hot guys!

她的建議好棒！對，我們應該要有些好玩的改變！這變得越來越有趣了！現在她讓我看到了為這次活動做主的好處了。如果我們可以決定，那我想跟其他部門的同事做在一起，我想要認識帥哥！

Wow! All Apple products to be our prizes, which are too good to be true! We are going to be the stars of this company if we really make all those things happen. This planning thing is way more fun than I thought!

哇！所有 Apple 的產品當獎品，好的太難以置信了吧！如果我們這得讓這些事都實現了，我們會成為這公司的偶像的。這個籌劃的事比我想像的好玩多了！

 Jung:

We are the ones who can plan for this year's annual banquet? I heard we can have a total control over it. I have always wanted to be responsible for our annual banquet. Finally!

我們是可以計畫今年尾牙的人嗎？我聽說我們可以有全權。我一直都想要負責我們的尾牙！終於！

Why is Margaret not thrilled about this? She hates planning that is why. Okay, then I will do a task allocation list, so it would be easier for her. I will give her the task allocation list today and ask her to meet me outside this week for discussion.

為什麼 Margaret 對此不興奮啊？原來她是討厭籌劃。好吧那我來做個工作分配表，那麼對她就會比較輕鬆。我會今天把工作分配表給她，然後叫她這禮拜跟我在外面討論。

Margaret is here now, I hope we can have everything organized soon, so we can get back to focus on work stuffs.

Margaret 在這裡了，希望我們可以快把所有事情組織起來，我們就可以趕快專心回到工作上。

She just wants to do the old stuffs, that is boring! I will let her hear out my ideas in mind first, and see if she is interested.

她只想做舊的東西，那很無聊！我要讓她先聽聽我的想法，看她有沒有興趣。

Good, now she is finally touched by me! I like her idea! This

Part 2

is what I am expecting for! Our ideas together really are too cool! Now let me tell her about prizes I am suggesting, I bet she will love this thought, too!

很好，現在她終於被我打動了！她現在的想法我喜歡！這就是我所期待的！我們的想法加在一起太酷了！現在讓我來跟她說我建議的獎項，我賭她也會愛這個想法！

 好好用句型

★ **As you know that our company draws for who is in charge of the annual banquet every year.**
如你們所知，我們公司每年是以抽籤的方式決定誰負責尾牙。
as you know
如你所知／據你所知

　Or you can say:
  ● as you are aware of
　據你所知道的
  ● based upon your understanding
　根據你所了解到、知道的

★ **Do we get to decide all the details?**
我們能夠決定所有細節嗎？
get to decide 能夠決定

　Or you can say:
  ● have a say
　有發言權（亦含有有權決定之意）
  ● have the right to decide
　有權利決定

★ **We can work this out together.**
我們可以一起想辦法
work it out 想辦法
Or you can say:
- figure it out
  弄清楚
- work it through
  想辦法解決

心理小測試

創造力測試

Q 假如你在新年的第一天去了寺廟求籤，你求得了一支上上籤，你看到大家都把上上籤掛在樹上，如果是你，你會選擇繫掛在什麼樣的樹枝上呢？

A：繫在高高的樹枝上，需要墊腳和手伸長才能抓到的

B：繫在一伸手就能碰到的樹枝上

C：繫在需要彎腰才能碰到的矮樹枝上

辦公室篇

貿易篇

業務篇

行銷篇

感情篇

測 驗 結 果

A：你是個有獨特思考方式的人，富有創造力的你常常讓周圍的人刮目相看。但是如果你的點子過於空想化而不現實，就有可能因為得不到別人的理解而被孤立。

B：你是個遵循常規的人，所以創造力也是合乎常情的，你常常得到別人的認同，你也同時對自己的工作能力有自信。在職場上，你通常不會有太大的失敗，但這樣同時也會被認為是墨守成規的人。

C：你是個習慣於被別人牽著鼻子走的人。你對於自己的判斷力缺乏自信，對於新的事物會有所抗拒，守舊是你的特質。

心理知識補一補

腦力激盪

　　腦力激盪（**Brainstorming**）依照現代心理學的定義為在團體中以集思廣益的方式徵求團體內所有人的意見，以解決現有的問題，而其有幾個特點是不同於一般的討論方式。

1. 徵求團體內所有人的意見愈多愈好。
2. 對於所提出的所有意見都會詳加紀錄，不論是否有符合主題。
3. 對於所提出的所有意見，在找出最佳的解決方式之前，並不加予評論。
4. 集結眾人的意見之後，再加予討論，除了選擇出最好的意見做為主體之外，還會利用其它的意見，來做擴充及修改。

　　在這個單元的對話中，因為只有 Margaret 和 Jung，所以並不能算是團體的腦力激盪。但可以看出來兩個人在對話中的討論其實相當符合以上所述的 Brainstorming 的 4 個要點。由第一個意見，引發出了一連串的討論及建議，進而讓意見更臻於完善，也讓原本不想負責的 Margaret 更有了參與感並且樂在其中。

辦公室篇

貿易篇

業務篇

行銷篇

感情篇

Part 3
業務篇

Unit 1 拜訪客戶 —菜鳥篇

前情提要

Nick and Avesh are on their way to visit a potential client. It is Avesh's first client visiting.

Nick 和 Avesh 在去拜訪一個潛在客戶的路上。這是 Avesh 的第一個客戶拜訪。

角色介紹

Avesh- The new salesperson（新手業務）

Nick- Avesh's colleague and also an experienced salesperson（Avesh 的同事，也同時是位有經驗的業務）

情境對話

Avesh: I am a bit nervous now. Later, when we see the client, do I start talking first or will you do that? What if I say something wrong and let us lose this potential client?

我現在有點緊張。等等我們見到客戶，我應該先開始說話嗎？還是你會這麼做？如果我說錯什麼話然後讓我們失去一個潛在客戶怎麼辦？

Nick: If you are that worried, I can do the opening for us. Relax, they won't bite! **I know you are not familiar with this,**

如果你這麼擔心，我可以替我們做個開場。放輕鬆，他們不會咬你！

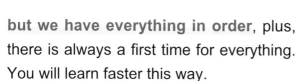

but we have everything in order, plus, there is always a first time for everything. You will learn faster this way.

我知道你對這個不熟悉，但是我們一切都準備好了，再加上，凡事都有第一次，而且你這樣會學得比較快。

Avesh: Okay, I will try to act normal and not to make it a big deal.
Can we maybe go over this client information and the standard of process again though?

好吧，那我會平常心，然後別把它看的太重。
我們可以再複習一次客戶資料還有標準程序嗎？

Nick: All the information you need is in that file you hold on your hand.
All we want is to sell our product and make a good impression on them.

所有你需要的資料都在你手上握著的資料夾裡。
我們要的就是賣產品還有給他們留下好印象。

Avesh: Okay, copy that!

好，收到！

Part 3

 前情提要

Nick accompanies Avesh to his first client visit.
Nick 陪著 Avesh 一起去他初次的客戶拜訪。

 角色介紹

Avesh- The new salesperson（新手業務）
Nick- Avesh's colleague and also an experienced salesperson
（Avesh 的同事，也同時是位有經驗的業務）
Andrea- The client（客戶）

 情境對話

Andrea: Hello, how may I help you?

你好，我可以怎麼幫你嗎？

Nick: Hi, we are the high-end printer provider, I know you must have printers already, but would you be interested in considering some of our printers? Perhaps it is time to replace your current one with a more efficient one, or just in case in the future, you might be looking for replacements.

您好，我們是高階印表機的供應商，我知道您們一定已經有印表機了，但是您會有興趣考慮一些我們的印表機嗎？也許您該是時候替換一個更有效率的印表機了，或者只是以防您們以後要找替代品。

Andrea: Sure, why not, do you have your catalog with you so we can look at?

當然，有何不可，你有帶你們的目錄可以給我們看嗎？

132

Nick: Yes, Avesh has it, and he will give you a brief introduction for all kinds that suit you.

有的，Avesh 有，而且他會為所有您們適合的印表機做一個簡單的介紹。

Avesh: Hi, this is our catalog, and these two are the best for your company, you can have a look and read it yourself, it is all on the paper.

您好，這是我們的目錄，然後這兩個是最適合您們公司的，您可以自己看一下、讀一下，都在這紙上了。

Andrea: Okay, thank you. **Wait, but I think you have got it wrong.**

好的，謝謝你。等等，但是我想你搞錯了。

Avesh: Sorry that is not the one, that is your company's profile.

抱歉這個不是，那是您們公司的檔案。

Nick: I am sorry, **he is really green.**

我很抱歉，他是新手。

Andrea: Ha ha! It is alright, it is cute!

哈哈！沒關係，很可愛！

辦公室心情隨筆

  Avesh:

I am so nervous I cannot breathe! I am so new, and now I have to deal with a real client. I do not know how to be persuasive yet and having Nick going with me is like having someone there to watch me. Will I be doing all the talking or will he help? What should I say other than "Hi" in the beginning?

我好緊張我不能呼吸了！我很嫩，然後我現在就要直接面對真實的客戶了。我還不知道要怎說服力，然後 Nick 跟我一起去就好像有人在那邊監視我一樣。我會要說所有話嗎還是他會幫忙？我一開始除了打招呼之外，還應該說什麼？

Nick is right, this is a great chance for me to learn and observe. I can finally learn and practice on my skills. I have all the information in hand, and there is nothing for me to worry about. He will back me up when I need. I hope I can make a good impression on them.

Nick 說得對，這事對我而言很好的學習還有觀察的機會。我終於可以學習還有練習我的技巧了。我有所有資料在手，也沒什麼是我該擔心的。我需要的時候他會支援我的。我希望我可以給他們留下好印象。

Okay, now Nick is doing the opening, should I just stand here and smile? Should I find a chance to talk or just be quite and act supportive?

好，現在 Nick 在做開場了，我是該就這樣笑著站在這裡嗎？我應該要找個機會說話，還是就安靜的表示支持就好？

Okay, now is my turn to impress this client. I will just give her our catalog, and she can reads herself. It is all written on the paper clearly. Oh, no. How come I handed the wrong paper to her? This should not have happened. Nick made me feel less embarrassed now.

好，現在換我來打動這個客戶了，我只要給她我們的目錄然後她就可以自己讀了，一切都很清楚寫在紙上。噢不。為什麼我拿錯紙給她？這真不應該發生。Nick 讓我感覺不那麼尷尬了。

Nick:

Avesh seems tense. He is just like me when I was at my first time, too. I did not have anyone accompany me for my first client visiting though, I still remembering being helpless when I was running out of words trying to sell our products.

Avesh 看起來緊張，他就像當初我第一次的時候一樣。但是我當時沒有人陪我去我的初次客戶拜訪，我還記得當我想試著賣我們產品的時候，那一種辭窮時的無助感。

I will help him to get through this, and he should be fine. We have all the details and selling points of the products written, and we have provided him the standard of process for him to follows. Now I just have to calm him down and tell him he is going to be alright.

我會幫他度過這個，而且他應該沒事的。我們有寫好的所有細節還有產品的賣點，然後我們還有標準程序給他照做。現在我只需要讓他冷靜下來，然後告訴他他會沒事的。

Okay, I am going to explain the reason why we are here to the lady first. Good that she is interested, and she is very kind to give us the chance to show her our printer line. People normally ignore us if they do not ungently in need for changing printers.

好，現在我要先跟這位小姐解釋我們來此的原因。還好她有興趣，她還給我機會給她看我們的印表機系列真好，通常人如果不是緊急需要換印表機都會忽略我們。

Okay, now I will pass the ball to Avesh, see if he can simply pick some printers that are right for this client and see if he knows how to sell them.

好，現在我要讓 Avesh 接下去，看他可不可以選出適合客戶的印表機，也看他知不知道怎麼推銷它們。

Did he just pass the client their own company profile? That is classic! A rookie mistake! Alright, at least he tried.

他剛剛是把客戶自己的公司檔案給她了嗎？這真經典！一個低級的錯誤！好吧，至少他試過了。

好好用句型

★ **I know you are not familiar with this, but we have everything in order.**

我知道你對這個不熟悉，但是我們一切都準備好了

everything in order 一切準備好了

Or you can say:

- Everything is in place.

一切準備好了。

- All setup.

一切準備好了。

★ **Wait, but I think you have got it wrong.**

等等，但是我想你搞錯了。

Got it wrong 搞錯了

Or you can say:

- Got it mistaken.

搞錯了。

- Made a mistake.
  弄錯了。

★ **I am sorry he is really green.**
我很抱歉，他是新手。
really green 新手／很菜
  Or you can say:
  - newbie
    新來的
  - rookie
    菜鳥

心理小測試

受同事非議程度

Q 假如今天公司要你們分組進行專案的討論，你會選擇和哪種人一起呢？

A：聰明且能提供好意見，但是常常堅持己見的人

B：活潑搞笑，但是都不太做事的人

C：擅於工作，但是驕傲的人

D：你最好的朋友，但是大家都不喜歡他

辦公室篇
貿易篇
業務篇
行銷篇
感情篇

測驗結果

A：受同事非議的程度有 **60%**。你在別人眼裡可能比較勢利眼，因此你不太被諒解，有時候甚至會被說成是雙面人或馬屁精。

B：受同事非議的程度有 **80%**。別人會覺得你想要不擇手段的當公司的風雲人物，而如果你真的是風雲人物，要小心別太驕傲惹人眼紅。

C：受同事非議的程度有 **40%**。你的個性可能有點固執，有時候你會怕能力比別人弱，甚至可能疑心病很重的懷疑別人，有些同事可能會受不了你這樣的個性，因而在背後議論你。

D：受同事非議的程度有 **20%**。你在同事眼中是個重情重義的人，無論別人對誰的看法如何，你總是對人很好。但是當好到一個偏心的程度的時候，就會被人議論。

心理知識補一補

潛在客戶

相信大家對於潛在客戶（**Potential Customer**）這一個名詞都相當的熟悉，這裡來簡單的介紹一下定義。潛在客戶指的是針對該產品或是服務有購買的慾望及有選擇購買的權力且有支付能力的人或是公司。

而潛在客戶的類型又可以大致地分為三種：

1. 新開發的潛在客戶：這類型的客戶，大多是由上司分配區域，由業務去拜訪開發，但也不乏是由現有的客戶中所介紹的。
2. 現有的客戶：除了產品維修保固之外，也應常拜訪這一些客戶，建立良好關係，這類型的客戶除了上述的會介紹新客戶之外，也是再次購買，或是購買新產品的主力客戶。
3. 終止往來的老客戶：這類型的客戶大概是業務最頭痛的部分，因為需要鼓起相當的勇氣才能去拜訪，建議在拜訪前先蒐集一些內部訊息，如是更換廠商的原因或是之前的一些業務記錄。也許在拜訪之後會發現只是單純的產品不適用等等的小問題，也許客戶也正在等著你去拜訪他呢。

辦公室篇

貿易篇

業務篇

行銷篇

感情篇

Unit 2 客戶拜訪—朋友篇

 前情提要

Lillian is paying a visit to an old client when she is free from a conference.

Lillian 趁著會議空檔去拜訪一個老客戶。

 角色介紹

Hager- A regular client of Lillian（Lillian 的一個老客戶）

Lillian- A salesperson（一位業務員）

 情境對話

Hager: Lillian! What brings you here?!

Lillian！什麼風把妳吹來了？！

Lillian: I am here for a conference, but also meeting some clients, while I am here.

我是為了會議而來的，但也順便趁我在這的時候拜訪客戶。

Hager: So you are not really here for me. I am so hurt.
Come on, how long has it been? It feels like forever.

所以妳不是真的為了我而來的。我好受傷。
拜託，我們有多久沒見了？感覺很久了。

Lillian: Of all the clients, I want to meet you and catch up with you the most. You know you are like a good friend to me. It is only been a year! That is probably because you miss me too much.

所有客戶之中，你是我最想見面和敘舊的。你知道你對我就像好朋友一樣。才過了一年！那是因為你太想我了。

Hager: True, I have missed you. We had so much fun talking last year.

對，我有想妳。我們去年聊得太開心了。

Lillian: Yes we did! Are you not going to pour me a cup of tea Hager? How rude!

對啊！Hager 你不幫我倒杯茶嗎？真沒禮貌！

Hager: Yeah, right! Lillian, can I get you a tea or coffee?

噢對！Lillian，我可以給妳咖啡還是茶嗎？

Lillian: I will have a tea, no sugar, just milk, thanks.
Hager what are you up to lately? I have actually stopped by for a several time last week, but I did not see you around.

我要一杯茶，不要糖，只要牛奶，謝謝。
Hager 你最近在忙些什麼？我其實上禮拜有來幾次，但是都沒看到你。

Hager: Do not mention it! It is a new project we have been working on. I am exhausted.

別提了！是一個我們正在進行的項目。我都筋疲力盡了。

Lillian: Let me cheer you up! I got something to show you.

我讓你振作起來! 我有東西要給你看。

Part 3

 前情提要

Lillian and Hager continue their conversation earlier.

Lillian 和 Hager 持續稍早的對話。

 角色介紹

Hager- A regular client of Lillian（Lillian 的一個老客戶）

Lillian- A salesperson（一位業務員）

 情境對話

Lillian: Check this out! I brought you your favorite pineapple cakes.

看看這個！我帶給你你最愛的鳳梨酥。

Hager: Lillian, no wonder I like you! This is exactly what I need for now.

Lillian，難怪我會喜歡妳！這正是我現在所需要的！

Lillian: Cool! Okay, now let us talk business! Last time, you proposed to integrate your system to our machines saying that you'll send me more details. How is that going right now?

酷！好，那現在我們來談生意吧！去年你提議要將你的系統和我們的機器整合，然後你說會寄給我更多細節。那個現在怎麼樣了？

Hager: Oh that! I am afraid I will have to kill the mood. It is not going to happen yet. Not yet. It is more complicated than we estimated.

噢那個！我很抱歉我要掃興了。這還沒有可能實現。還沒。它比我們預估的還要複雜。

Lillian: How so? I thought as long as they can communicate…

怎麼說？我以為只要它們可以互通……

Hager: Yeah, that was what we believed too, but it turned out that our system does not support the platform of your machine, and it will still require a lot of work.

對，我們也是那樣認為，但事實證明我們的系統不支援妳們機器的平台，而且還需要大量的努力。

Lillian: What a pity! I thought we can see some results by the end of the year. It is still executable and possible right?

可惜！我還以為我們在今年年底前可以看到一些結果。它仍然是可執行的也是有可能的，對嗎？

Hager: Yes it is. Just need more time.

是的。只是還需要些時間。

Lillian: We have got time. We can wait!

我們有時間，我們可以等！

Part 3

辦公室心情隨筆

Lillian:

Since we are going there, I have to spare some time to visit Hager, and I am not giving him a head up. I will just show up by surprise. I will bring his favorite pineapple cake with me, so he will be more thrilled.

既然我們要去那邊，我一定要空出些時間去探望 Hager，然後我不要先告訴他。我要就這麼出現給他驚喜。我會帶他對愛的鳳梨酥，那他就會更興奮。

He is really surprised, and I can tell that he misses me. It has been a year, but he is still the same, it is like we can never end our conversation. It is good that I finally see him now because the last few times last week I missed him.

他真的很訝異而且我看得出來他有想我。一年了，但他還是一樣，就好像我們的話題永遠無法結束一樣。終於看到他了真好，因為上禮拜幾次我都錯過他了。

He is working on a new project, no wonder he looks tired. I will give him the present I prepared for him later, so he can give me a bigger smile.

他在進行一個新的項目，難怪他看起來累。我等下要給他我為他準備的禮物，他就會給我更大的笑容。

I knew he would love it! He cannot resist the charm of our pineapple cake.

我就知道他會喜歡！他無法抗拒鳳梨酥的魅力。

Okay, now I am going to check the progress of his proposal last year.

好，現在我要問問他去年的提議的進度了。

Too bad the technique is not that mature yet, I thought it

is easy to do the integration.

技術還不成熟真可惜，我以為做這個整合很容易。

It is alright, I can wait because it's better than nothing. Besides, it then gives me another excuse to come back here.

沒關係，我可以等，因為有總比沒有好。再說，這樣還可以給我另一個回來這裡的藉口。

Hager:

Wow! Is that Lillian? I miss her! I cannot believe she is here and I happen to need some company. She always looks so energetic. It has been a long time since I saw her last time. When was that? Years? What? Is it only last year? She is still funny, and she still has her tea that way.

哇！那是 Lillian 嗎？我想她了！我不敢相信她在這，而且我正需要有人陪。她總是看起來那麼有活力。距離我上次見到她好久了。那是什麼時候？好多年了？什麼？才一年嗎？她還是那麼幽默，然後她喝茶習慣還是那樣。

Wow! My love! Pineapples from Taiwan! How nice of her! It is so sweet that she still remembers that I love it as I only mentioned her once from last year. Also, it is like the only one thing that can brighten me up now!

哇！我的愛！台灣的鳳梨酥！她真好！她還記得我愛這個很貼心，因為我只在去年跟她提過一次。還有，這大概是現在唯一一個可以振奮我的東西！

Now the business talks! Oh yeah I forgot to update her about that. I should tell her which step we are in. I am glad that she brings this up now, so I can let her know the plan. I hope she gets how many hard work and testing we need to do

before it is done though she does not know this area. She is a
bit disappointed I can see, but like she said, we have time.

現在談生意！噢對我忘了跟她說最新進度了。我應該告訴她我們現
在在哪個階段的。我很高興她現在提起了，我就可以讓她知道這計劃。
我希望她明白在做成之前是需要很多作業和測試的，雖然她不懂這塊。
她有點失望我看得出來，但就如她所說的，我們有時間。

 ## 好好用句型

★ **I have actually stopped by for a several time last week but I
did not see you around.**

我其實上禮拜有來幾次，但是都沒看到你。

stop by 順路/順道拜訪/路過

Or you can say:

- drop by

  順道拜訪

- swing by

  順道拜訪（有快速拜訪之意）

★ **I am afraid I will have to kill the mood.**

我很抱歉我要掃興了。

kill the mood 掃興

Or you can say:

- bummer, what a bummer

  掃興／真掃興

- spoil the fun, spoilsport

  掃興／掃興的人

★ **It turned out that our system does not support the platform of your machine**

但事實證明我們的系統不支援你們機器的平台

it turns out 事實證明

Or you can say:

- prove the facts / facts proved

  事實證明

- make a case / a case can be made

  事實證明

 心理小測試

職場老油條

Q 假如你不小心開錯了一扇門，相較之下，你最寧願你開錯的是以下哪扇門？

A：恐怖的地獄之門

B：老虎籠子的門

C：精神病院病患的門

D：殘暴食人族的門

測驗結果
請見下頁

測驗結果

A：老油條指數 20%。你對於人際關係保持著平和的態度。當你還是新人的時候，你就已經會不喜歡總是倚老賣老的人。在你心中，沒什麼比真誠更重要。

B：老油條指數 50%。你是很公私分明的，在工作中就很專業且老道，但私下卻又是同事的開心果，能跟同事打成一片，你是讓大家感覺不出來的老油條。

C：老油條指數 90%。你很愛碎碎念，很愛把自己的經驗講給新人或是犯錯的人聽。

D：老油條指數 0%。你完全活在自己的世界裡，不管你到幾歲，你的內心永遠會保持像新鮮人一樣，你不講究什麼人情世故，做事情一向對事不對人。你認為勾心鬥角從不是你的事。

心理知識補一補

情感協調

　　在行銷心理學中，如何跟客戶產生「情感協調」是一門重要的學問，這裡說的不是與客戶產生男女間的感情或是，或是為客戶的情感問題做斡旋、協調。而是要如何跟客戶拉近距離，甚至是有一見如故的感覺。

　　在職場的人際關係中，以顧客與廠商之間總是會巧妙地形成一種互信互助，但往往也會是彼此警惕的關係，就像是在對話當中 Lillian 與 Hager 的關係。兩人之間的相處雖然已經像是老友一般，但在談到類似公事的時候總也會多一份戒心。而 Lillian 在這一次的拜訪中，除了寒暄之外，還記住了 Hager 的喜好，為他帶了一盒鳳梨酥，成功地化解了 Hager 在心中默默吶喊的 "Not another work-related thing, please!"。使得接下來的 business talk 就顯得平和，也更有效率。

　　其實類似這樣的話術，我們常會不自覺地用在日常生活當中，例如是像是對於初次見面的人，會詢問對方是哪裡人？哪個學校畢業的？以尋求與對方之間的共同點，進而拉近彼此的心理距離，也為未來的良好相處鋪下契機。

辦公室篇

貿易篇

業務篇

行銷篇

感情篇

Unit 3 嚇死人不償命簡報

 前情提要

Angelina is making a presentation in front of the board of directors tomorrow, and she is asking her manager- Brad for advice.

Angelina 明天要在董事會面前做簡報,她在問她的主管的建議。

 角色介紹

Brad- A manager of Angelina(Angelina 的主管)

Angelina- The speaker(演講者)

 情境對話

Brad: Tomorrow is the day! Are you ready for the meeting briefing?

就是明天了!妳準備好會議簡報了嗎?

Angelina: **I have never given such an important brief before, let alone giving presentations in such a big meeting.** I have been staying up late for it, but I am still so nervous, can you give me some tips?

我從沒有做過這麼重要的簡報,更別說是在這麼重要的會議裡面做簡報。我為此都在熬夜,但我還是好緊張,你可以給我一些訣竅嗎?

Brad: Well, you have to check the equipment and your PowerPoint slides

這個嘛,妳必須在妳進去前檢查好設備還有妳的

before you go in, and basically the PowerPoint slides should be your biggest assistance, you have to keep to the point and use figures, charts, and graphs well.

PowerPoint 投影片,基本上 PowerPoint 投影片應該是妳最大的助手,妳必須講重點,善用數據和圖表。

You just have to use PowerPoint effectively. You should have an outline on your first slide, Do not use too many words per slide, because people are more comfortable seeing visuals not a bunch of texts, and the font size cannot be smaller than 28.

妳就是要有效使用 PowerPoint。在第一頁要有大綱,每張投影片別用太多文字,因為人是看到圖像比一堆文字舒服的,然後字體不能小於 28。

Angelina: So a perfect PowerPoint will do?

所以一個完美的 PowerPoint 就好了?

Brad: That is not entirely true. **Having the PowerPoint right is not enough, it also depends on the way you present it**. You have to be confident and interesting during your presentation, some interactions are great, too. A lot of practices will do.

那不完全是對的。有正確的 PowerPoint 是不夠的,還要靠妳呈現的方式。在妳的演講中,妳必須有自信和有趣,做些互動也很好。多做練習就對了。

Angelina: You are right! Practice makes perfect.

你說的對!熟能生巧。

Brad: Now you got it!

現在妳明白了!

Part 3

After Angelina gave the presentation, she is now asking Brad about his thought.

在 Angelina 簡報完之後，她現在在問 Brad 他的想法。

 角色介紹

Brad: A manager of Angelina（Angelina 的主管）
Angelina: The speaker（演講者）

 情境對話

Angelina: How was I up there?　　　　我在上面表現如何？

Brad: You tell me! That was a total disaster! You did not speak loud enough and you kept stammering. Moreover, the structure is awful, and the font size is too small and some of your graphs did not show. Also, you used too many effects which were very confusing.

妳說呢！那簡直是場災難！妳講得不夠大聲而且妳一直吃螺絲。再說，妳的架構糟糕，字體太小，然後有些妳的圖沒有顯示出來。還有，妳用太多動態效果了，讓人覺得混亂。

Angelina: I do not know what happened to me. I did practice. I thought my PowerPoint was good. Did you like the background music I put in? I edited that music myself.

我不知道我怎麼了。我有練習。我以為 PowerPoint 很好。你喜歡我放的背景音樂嗎？我自己剪輯那個音樂的。

Brad: The music did not fit the topic, and it did not sound professional.

那個音樂不適合主題，聽起來也不專業。

Why are there so many pages? I do not know if you have noticed they got bored. Besides, I told you to keep watch on the time, it was a 15 minutes presentation, but have you realized you took 35 minutes? You just lost yourself there, just went on and on, it was already time for lunch, and you had to let them remind you that your time was up.

為什麼有那麼多頁？我不知道妳有沒有注意他們感到無聊了。此外，我告訴妳要注意時間，這是個 15 分鐘的簡報，但是妳有發現妳花了 35 分鐘嗎？妳就講到忘我了，一直講一直講，已經是午餐時間了，妳還要讓他們提醒妳時間到了。

Angelina, I expected more from you. I thought you could impress them and me, **but you just let the chance slip by.**

Angelina，我對妳有更多期望的，我以為妳會讓我還有他們驚艷，但妳在剛剛讓機會流失了。

Angelina: Sorry.

對不起。

Part 3

 Brad:

Tomorrow is the day for the briefing, and Angelina will represent us in front of the board. I believed in her but let me go check on her.

明天就是簡報會議的日子了，Angelina 在董事會面前代表我們。我相信她但是我去看看她好了。

She looks nervous, and I can see she has not been sleeping much. Okay, I will provide her some useful tips on making presentations and some basic requirements for PowerPoint making. I think I have given her a clear guidance already. As long as she has enough practices, she can make it.

她看起來是緊張的，而且我可以看得出她最近沒怎麼睡，好的，我會給她一些有用的簡報秘訣，還有一些做 PowerPoint 的基本要求。我想我已經給她很清楚的指導了。只要她有足夠的練習，她可以做到的。

Now is Angelina's turn for making the presentation.

現在輪到 Angelina 作簡報了。

I cannot even hear her voice, and she can hardly finish a sentence up there.

我根本聽不到她的聲音，而且她根本在台上說不出完整的句子。

What is wrong with the PowerPoint slides? I cannot read the texts and why do I see pictures not showing up there? Now the time is out, and what is she still doing there?

那些 PowerPoint 投影片是怎麼了？我看不到字而且為什麼我看到有些圖片沒有顯示出來？現在超過時間了，她還在那邊幹嘛？

Now she is asking about my thoughts. I will not hide any of my feelings and comments; I must let her know how unsatisfied I am.

現在她在問我我的想法，我不會隱瞞任何我的感覺還有看法的，我一定要讓她知道我有多不滿意。

Yeah, now she reminds me about the music, the music is unnecessary. Why take the trouble to do that?

對，現在她提醒了我那個音樂，那個音樂就像是不必要的。何必多此一舉呢？

The apology is not accepted and does not change anything.

這道歉根本是不能接受的也不會改變任何事。

 Angelina:

Since Brad is here now, I should ask some tips from him as he is the expert on making presentations. His presentations are never boring. I must ask him to share his secrets to it.

既然 Brad 現在在這裡，我應該向他問一些訣竅，因為他是做簡報的專家，他的簡報從不枯燥無味。我一定要他分享給我其中的秘密。

So what he says is as long as I make a perfect PowerPoint, I will have nothing to worry about? Oh, right, how you deliver the presentation is truly crucial. I have done a couple of good presentations before, I should be fine. I have done so many practices on this. I just need some more practices before the presentation, that is all I need.

所以他說的意思是只要我做出完美的 PowerPoint，我就沒有什麼擔心的了？噢對，怎麼樣呈現簡報是很重要的。我之前有做過幾個好的簡報，我應該會沒事的。我有做那麼多練習了，我只需要在簡報之前多做一些練習，這就是我所需要的。

Oh no, how come some of the graphics are not displaying? They were fine on my computer. Is there something wrong with this computer or what? What? Is it 15 minutes already? I have not yet finished my presentation and I have not yet go through each slide yet, there is more at the back. No! Looks like I have to finish like this.

　　噢不，為什麼有些圖表沒有顯示出來呢？它們在我電腦裡面的時候都好好的。是這台電腦有什麼問題嗎還是什麼？什麼？已經 15 分鐘了嗎？我還沒完成我的簡報，我也還沒講完每一張的投影片，後面還有。不！看來我要這樣結束了。

Brad is there, let me see what he thinks. Okay, I let him down and he is so right for each point. I am sorry, but it is not helping.

　　Brad 在那裡，我要看看他怎麼想。好，我讓他失望了，而且他說的都對。我感到抱歉，但是這幫不到什麼。

好好用句型

★ **I have never given such an important brief before, let alone giving presentations in such a big meeting.**
我從沒有做過這麼重要的簡報，更別說是在這麼重要的會議裡面做簡報。

let alone
更不用說、更別提

　　Or you can say:
　　● Much less （更不用說）
　　● Not to mention （更別提）

★ **Having the PowerPoint right is not enough; it also depends on the way you present it.**
有正確的 PowerPoint 是不夠的，還要靠你呈現的方式。
it depends on

隨……而定（也有依賴／依靠之意）

Or you can say:

- It relies on

  隨……而定

- It differs from

  依照不同情況而定

★ **I thought you could impress me and them, but you just let the chance slip by.**

我以為你會讓我還有他們驚艷，但你在剛剛讓機會流失了。

Let the chance slip by.

讓機會流失、失去機會。

Or you can say:

- Let the opportunity slip away.

  讓機會流失。

- Let something slip through one's finger.

  痛失良機。

辦公室篇

貿易篇

業務篇

行銷篇

感情篇

心理小測試

你的警覺性

Q 假如今天你在坐飛機時，突然感受到很強烈的震動，你開始隨著機身劇烈的左右搖晃。此時的你，會怎麼做呢？

A：繼續看電影或閱讀或睡覺，不太在意正在發生的騷動

B：注意情況的變化，仔細聽播音員的播音，並翻看一下緊急情況應變手冊，以防萬一

C：手足無措，很慌張

D：不能確定，或者根本沒注意到騷動

測驗結果
請見下頁

測驗結果

A：你對危機出現時表現出了一定的冷靜，但是警覺性不高。

B：你表現出了在危機下冷靜且理智的處理方式。

C：有足夠的警覺，但有時候會太過於緊張，且有過份神經質的傾向。

D：你像溫水裡面煮的青蛙一般，對於外界的變化和壓力都十分麻木。

辦公室篇

貿易篇

業務篇

行銷篇

感情篇

Unit 4 出國參展 魅力大放送

 前情提要

Joy is checking with Jimmy about their booth in an international trade show and discussing who to attend this show with Jimmy. Ben overheard their conversation and join their conversation from there.

Joy 在跟 Jimmy 核對關於他們一個國際展覽上的攤位，以及討論誰要和 Jimmy 去參加這場展覽，Ben 聽到了他們的對話後，就加入了他們的對話。

 角色介紹

Joy- Jimmy's manager（Jimmy 的主管）
Jimmy- A experienced sales（一個業務）
Ben- A new sales（一個新業務）

 情境對話

Joy: Jimmy, have you finished the registration of our booth yet?
Jimmy 你完成我們攤位的註冊了嗎？

Jimmy: Yes, right at the ideal location that you asked for.
有，就正在你要求的理想的位置裡面。

Joy: Well done. Have you applied for
做的好。你有申請額外兩

additional two electrical outlets for our booth?

個插座給我們的攤位了嗎？

Jimmy: Yes and they said it would be free since we book the booth early.

有的。而且他們還説會是免費，因為我們早訂攤位。

Joy: Good to know! What did I tell you! **The early bird catches the worm!**

太好了！我就跟你説吧！早起的鳥兒有蟲吃！

Joy: Do you think you can take Ben with you this time so he can practice? **I will probably pass.**

你覺得你可以帶 Ben 跟你一起去嗎？他就可以練習，我應該就不去了。

Jimmy: No, you must join me, and Ben can go next time when he is more experienced.

不行，你一定要一起去，而且 Ben 可以等下次他比較有經驗的時候再去。

Jimmy: He could not even handle the national exhibition last month, and now you are putting him to this huge trade show?

他都處理不了上個月國內的展覽了，而你現在要放他到這個大型商展嗎？

Joy: Yeah right. Now I recall it. Thanks for reminding me, Jimmy.

噢對。現在我想起來了。謝謝你提醒我啊，Jimmy。

Ben: I am sorry to interrupt, but Joy **can you allow me to attend this once in a life time show?** I am aware that this

我很抱歉打斷，但是 Joy，你可以允許我去參加這個千載難逢的展覽

Part 3

show only happens every 4 years. I can learn from Jimmy's marketing skills. Also, I am very confident in my English.

嗎？我知道這個展覽每 4 年只有一次。我可以從 Jimmy 那邊學銷售技巧。還有，我對我的英文非常有自信。

Joy: Okay, you just got yourself a ticket in.

好，你為你自己得到進去的門票了。

Ben: Thank you so much, Joy.

非常謝謝你，Joy。

 前情提要

Jimmy and Ben are now at the international trade show. They soon have Mimi step into their booth asking for introducing a product.

Jimmy 和 Ben 現在在國際展覽上了，很快 Mimi 就會走進他們的攤位並要求他們介紹產品了。

 角色介紹

Jimmy- A experienced sales.（一個業務）
Ben- A new sales.（一個新業務）
Mimi- A visitor from a trade show（一個商展上的參觀者）

 情境對話

Jimmy: Now our booth is all set up, in 15 minutes the visitors will be allowed to get in.

現在我們的攤位都設好了，在 15 分鐘後參觀者就可以允許入場了。

I know you got your degrees oversea, but I have taken many English classes, too.

我知道你在海外得到你的學位的，但是我也有上很

162

Allow me to do all the talking, you can help out when I ask you to, alright?

多堂英文課。讓我負責說話，等我叫你幫忙你就可以幫忙，好嗎？

Ben: Sure, not a problem at all.

當然，根本不成問題。

Mimi: I like this design here. I just walk in, and this iPhone casing just immediately caught my eye. Can someone give me some background information and some introduction please?

我喜歡這裡這個設計，我才剛走進來就被這個 iPhone 的殼吸引了我的目光。有人可以拜託給我一些背景資訊還有一些產品介紹嗎？

Jimmy: This is our brand new design from our team… and… it is…
Ben will tell you more.

這是我們團隊全新的設計……還有……這是……
Ben 會告訴您更多。

Ben: Good morning, ma'am.

早安，女士。

Mimi: Just call me Mimi.

叫我 Mimi 就好了。

Ben: Okay, Mimi. You are now looking at our new cutting-edge iPhone case. It is designed from our creative team in Taiwan, and it is not just good looking, but also very light and practical. Besides, this casing is made of environmentally friendly materials.

好的，Mimi。您在看的是我們新的尖端的 iPhone 殼，是由我們台灣的創意團隊所設計的，而且不只好看，也同時非常地輕還有實用，此外，這個殼還是由環保材料製成的。

辦公室篇
貿易篇
業務篇
行銷篇
感情篇

Part 3

Mimi: Very tempting! Who says we cannot have it all, right?

非常誘人！誰說魚與熊掌不能兼得，對吧？

Ben: Exactly! Mimi, do you have any more questions for me?

沒錯！Mimi 您還有要問我什麼問題嗎？

Mimi: Not for now, Ben, I want to meet you tomorrow for further details on cooperation.

現在沒有，Ben，我想明天為了合作的進一步細節和你碰面。

Ben: No problem.

沒問題。

 辦公室心情隨筆

Jimmy:

Joy should not have to worry about me organizing an international trade show. It is not like it is my first show. However, he is right to ask me to get the whole registration thing done early in the first place. I thought it was too early to apply.

Joy 不該擔心我關於一個國際商展的籌劃。又不是說這是我的第一場展覽。然而他一開始就要我早把整個註冊的事情弄好是對的。我以為太早申請了。

I do not want to take Ben with me. I still remember he's not talking at all in the booth last month. I do not see how he will be good at this international trade show. Joy, on the other hand, can make big decisions at the show and he speaks good English, too. To make this trade show perfect, Joy should be the one to go with me. I think I can really use his help at the show.

　　我不想帶 Ben 跟我一起去，我還記得他上個月在攤位上都完全不講話，我看不出他在這國際商展能做好。Joy 就另當別論了，他在展覽上可以做重大決定的，Joy 應該是那個跟我去的人。我想我在展場上真的會需要他的幫忙。

Ben just cut into our conversation like that. That is why I do not like him. He really wants to go to this show and Joy just said yes to him, just like that. Okay, then. What can I say? We will see.

　　Ben 就這樣插進我們的對話了。這就是為什麼我不喜歡他。他真的想去這個展覽，然後 Joy 就跟他說好了，就那樣。好吧。我能說什麼呢？我們等著看。

Now, just waiting for the show to get started. Let me get things straight to Ben.

　　現在，只等展覽開始了。讓我把事情跟 Ben 說清楚。

Okay, now we have one visitor. But, I do not know what to say now. I need Ben.

　　好，現在我們有一個參觀者。但我現在不知道要說什麼了。我需要 Ben。

 Ben:

Are they talking about me? Jimmy is not recommending me to Joy. I have always wanted to go to this international trade as it is rare, and who knows whether in 4 years I will still be here or not. Jimmy just looks me down. I have to talk to Joy before he makes the final decision. Also, I didn't do well on the exhibition last month, and Joy must have a bad impression on me, too. This is my chance to impress him. Okay,

Part 3

I am going to stop their conversation now and sell myself to Joy.

他們是在講我嗎？Jimmy 不把我推薦給 Joy。我一直都想去這個國際展，因為很少，而且誰知道 4 年後我會不會還在這裡。Jimmy 就是瞧不起我。我必須在 Joy 做最後決定前跟他說到話。還有，我在上個月的展覽表現不好，Joy 應該也對我印象不好，這是我給他留下好印象的機會。好，我現在要去打斷他們的對話，然後向 Joy 推銷自己了。

I did it! That was easy! So that is why I always believe that if you do not ask, you do not get. Hope I can get along with Jimmy. I will show him what I have got and make him regret of not wanting me. I will prove him wrong!

我做到了！還蠻簡單的！這就是為什麼我總是相信，你不爭取就得不到。希望我可以跟 Jimmy 好好相處。我要給他看我的本事，然後讓他後悔不要我。我會証明他是錯的！

Okay, now the booth is ready. There is a lady walking toward us. Jimmy starts to do the talking. Now there he is! He is running out of line now. Like he said, I will only step in when he asks me to. Okay, now is my turn. Show time!

好，現在攤位都好了。那裡有個小姐朝著我們走過來。Jimmy 開始講話了。現在他那樣！他沒有台詞好說了。就如他所說的，我只會在他叫我的時候才過去。好，現在換我了。好戲上場！

好好用句型

★ **Good to know! What did I tell you! The early bird catches the worm!**

太好了！我就跟你說吧！早起的鳥兒有蟲吃！

The early bird catches （gets） the worm.

早起的鳥兒有蟲吃。／捷足先登。

Or you can say:

- First come, first served.
  先到先服務。（有先到先贏及捷足先登之意）
- They beat us to it.
  他們捷足先登了。

★ **I will probably pass.**
我應該就不去了。
I will pass.
我就不去了。

  Or you can say:
  - I am not going. / I am not coming.
    我就不去了。
  - Count me out.
    別算我一份。（即有我不去了之意）

★ **Can you allow me to attend this once in a life time show?**
你可以允許我去參加這個千載難逢的展覽嗎？
Once in a life time 千載難逢
Or you can say:
  - It is now or never.（趁現在，不然永遠沒機會了。即有千載難逢之意。）
  - Once in a blue moon.（千載難逢）

心理小測試

你的天賦在哪裡？

Q 假如你今天趕著搭電梯，你因為晚了一步而沒趕上。請回想一下，通常這時候的你在等下一班電梯時，你最常表現出以下哪種行為呢？

A：忍不住一直按按鈕好幾次

B：有時候會在地上跺腳

C：抬頭看天花板

D：看著地上

E：盯著樓層指示燈，然後等門一開便立刻衝進去

測驗結果
請見下頁

測驗結果

A：你注重選擇，有時候沉迷其到渾然忘我。你人緣很好，有公
　　關方面的天賦。

B：你感情敏銳，能憑直覺洞察他人，具有藝術天賦。

C：你心地善良，有數學才能，在理工科方面有天賦。

D：這種行為有兩種類型。一種是做人消極，不喜歡袒露心跡；
　　另一種則是與此相反，是個坦率且人際關係好的人。

E：你小心謹慎，不做冒險的事情。若做領導的工作，能深得屬
　　下愛戴，但可能過於理性。

辦公室篇

貿易篇

業務篇

行銷篇

感情篇

Unit 5 膠囊商旅

 前情提要

Jingle and Siobhan are going to an exhibition in England, but they just found out they will be staying in capsule hotels.

Jingle 和 Siobhan 要去一個英國的展覽，但他們剛剛發現他們要住在膠囊旅店裡。

 角色介紹

Amy- The supervisor of Jingle and Siobhan（Jingle 和 Siobhan 的主管）

Jingle- Sales 1（業務 1）

Siobhan- Sales 2（業務 2）

 情境對話

Amy: Jingle and Siobhan, do you want to go and check out this year's exhibition in England?

Jingle 和 Siobhan，你們想去看看今年在英國的展覽嗎？

Jingle: **Anything you say.**

一切都聽你的。

Siobhan: I thought we are not exhibiting.

我以為我們沒有要展覽。

Amy: Yes, but we can still see what others are doing. Get some ideas and be

是啊，但是我們還是可以看看其他人在幹嘛。得到

inspired.

一些想法和啟發。

Siobhan: Why say no to a free trip? Okay I will contact a travel agency for the ticket and accommodation arrangements. Jingle can you go online to register for us?

幹嘛要跟免費之旅説不？好，那我會連絡旅行社安排機票和住宿。Jingle 你可以去網路上幫我們註冊嗎？

Jingle: I just did. Now we only require a ticket and a room to sleep.

我剛弄完了。現在只需要一張票和一間睡覺的房間。

Siobhan: Oh no! Since it is too last minute, all rooms nearby are fully-booked and tickets are sold out too. Our only option is to take the capsule hotels.

噢不！因為太臨時了，所有附近的房間都滿了，然後票也賣光了。我們唯一的選擇是膠囊旅店。

Jingle: Capsule hotels are fine with me, not a problem. How about air tickets?

膠囊旅店對我而言是可以的，不是個問題。那麼機票呢？

Siobhan: They said unless we leave tonight, or there will be no seats at all.

他們説除非我們今晚就離開，否則沒有任何位子給我們。

Jingle: I can have my bags packed and be wheels up by 9. How about you?

到 9 點我就能收拾好行李整裝待發了。那妳呢？

Siobhan: Leaving tonight is alright, but I do not feel like staying in a capsule hotel.

今晚離開是可以的，但是我不想待在膠囊旅店。

辦公室篇

貿易篇

業務篇

行銷篇

感情篇

Part 3

Jingle: Come on! It is not that bad! **Are you expecting 5 star hotels at this stage?**

拜託！並沒有那麼糟！事到如今妳還期待五星級酒店嗎？

Siobhan: Okay then.

好吧。

 前情提要

Now Jingle and Siobhan just arrived England and finished checking in, they are on their way to their rooms now.

現在 Jingle 和 Siobhan 到了英國也登記入住完了，他們現在在去他們房間的路上。

 角色介紹

Jingle: Sales 1（業務 1）
Siobhan: Sales 2（業務 2）

 情境對話

Siobhan: Let us go see our room now.

現在讓我們去看我們房間吧。

Siobhan: Oh my! They are like cages for pets. Are those seriously our rooms?

我的天啊！它們就像寵物的籠子一樣。這真是我們的房間嗎？

Jingle: Yes. They are tiny but delicate. Be calm, and take things as they come.

是的。它們小但是精緻。冷靜點，既來之則安之吧。

辦公室篇

Siobhan: Here smells bad and right now I can hear the guy next to me snoring.

這裡聞起來怪怪的，而且現在我可以聽到隔壁的人在打呼。

貿易篇

Jingle: **Live with it, Siobhan!** We are only staying here for 2 nights.
Did you see their executive lounge at front? It is big and they have many facilities there.
They let us pick our own check-out time, which is quite special.

忍受吧，Siobhan！我們只在這裡待 2 個晚上。
妳有看到他們前面的交誼廳嗎？很大而且有很多設施。
他們還讓我們選退房時間，是蠻特別的。

業務篇

Siobhan: Who cares about a fancy executive lounge? I cannot even stay in my cage for more than 5 minutes. Also, I would like to check out early in the morning, so I can smell fresh air soon.

誰在乎精美的交誼廳啊？我根本不能待在我的籠子裡超過 5 分鐘。還有，我想要一大早退房，我就可以聞到新鮮空氣了。

行銷篇

Jingle: If you do not like what is in the hotel, think outside! We are like the closet hotel to their biggest shopping mall. Is not that something you love?

如果妳不喜歡旅店裡面，想想外面！我們大概是離他們最大的購物中心最近的飯店了。這不是妳會愛的事情嗎？

感情篇

Siobhan: Really? In that case, this has just become a good accommodation!

真的嗎？如果是這樣的話，這就在剛剛成為了一個好的住宿。

Part 3

辦公室心情隨筆

Jingle:

Finally, Amy brings this up! Of course, I want to go to England! Not exhibiting this year is sad enough, at least I want them to let me attend the show. Okay, now Siobhan is handling our tickets and accommodation, I will go do online registration, I will get it done before she asks.

Amy 終於提起這個了！我當然想去英國！今年不展出已經夠難過了，至少我想要他們讓我去參加展覽。好，現在 Siobhan 在處理我們的機票和住宿了，我去線上註冊，在她叫我做之前我就會先做好。

Capsule hotels only? It is alright, it is better than nothing. How about plane tickets? I am easy because I do not have much to pack. It is totally fine for me to leave tonight. How come Siobhan is that picky? She should not forget our purpose for the trip and if she is not that willing to stay at places rather than nice hotels, she can choose to stay here.

只有膠囊旅店？這是可以的，總比沒有好。那麼機票呢？我很簡單的我沒有很多要打包的，今晚就要離開對我來說完全沒問題。為什麼 Siobhan 這麼挑剔？她不該忘了我們這趟旅行的目的，還有如果她這麼不願意住在不是好飯店的地方，他可以選擇留在這裡。

Okay, now it is time to see our rooms. It is not that bad, it is clean and tidy, and it is got everything we need. I hope she can just face the fact that she has nowhere else to go but here. Let me try to calm her down by telling the advantages of this hotel. Okay, it is not working. How about that big shopping mall? That might attract her? Now she likes it.

好，現在到了看我們房間的時間了。沒那麼糟，是乾淨整齊的，還有所有我們需要的東西。我希望她能面對她沒有其它地方可以去了的事實。讓我試這以告訴她這家旅店的優點而讓她冷靜下來吧。好吧，沒有效。那麼那個大的購物商場呢？那有可能吸引她嗎？現在她喜歡了。

 Siobhan:

Amy wants us to go? I will not only go there for business. I want to do some shopping when I got some free time, too. After all it is England we are talking about. I hope it is not too late for us to book our rooms and tickets. I will ask Jingle to do the registration for the show, while I contact our travel agency. Oh, he is quick! No! No hotels? Only capsule hotels? I am never a fan of it! Jingle is okay with capsule hotels? Why? We have to leave tonight? I need a lot of time for packing, but he can be ready that soon? Okay then, if Jingle put it that way, I can only be okay, too.

Amy 想要我們去嗎？我不會只是為了公事而去。當我有空閒時間的時候我要購物。畢竟我們在講的是英國。我希望訂機票和房間不會太晚。我會叫 Jingle 趁我在跟我們旅行社連絡的時候註冊。噢，他真快！不！沒飯店？只有膠囊旅店？我從來就不喜歡它！Jingle 覺得膠囊旅店可以嗎？為什麼？我們今晚就要離開嗎？我需要很多時間打包，為什麼他可以那麼快準備好？好吧，如果 Jingle 都那樣說了，我也只能說好了。

Okay, we are here in England now. The next stop would be the capsule hotel. Please do not be so bad! Oh no! This is bad! Are we dogs and cats or what? They are keeping us in those spaces like pets. This is way beyond my limit! What is that smell and sound? Jingle is trying hard to make me like it. Oh! The biggest shopping mall is near us? Not that bad then!

好，我們現在在英國了。下一站就是膠囊旅店了。拜託別太糟！噢不！這好糟！我們是狗還是貓還是什麼嗎？他們把我們放在那些空間裡面像寵物一樣。這遠超過我的極限了！那是什麼味道還有聲音？Jingle 努力想讓我喜歡它！噢！最大的購物中心在我們附近嗎？那其實沒那麼糟嘛！

好好用句型

★ **Anything you say.**
   一切都聽你的。

   Or you can say:
   - It's your call.
     由你下決定。（也有「一切都聽你的」之意）
   - I am all yours.
     我都是你的。（有任你宰割之意，也含有一切都聽你的意思）

★ **Are you expecting 5 star hotels at this stage?**
   事到如今你還期待五星級酒店嗎？
   at this stage 事到如今/眼下／現階段

   Or you can say:
   - under the circumstances
     事到如今/在這種情況下
   - by now
     事到如今

★ **Live with it, Siobhan!**
   忍受吧，**Siobhan！**
   live with it
   勉強接受吧；忍受吧

   Or you can say:

- Get along with it.

  忍受吧；勉強接受吧！
- Deal with it!

  妥協吧！

 心理小測試

職場個性特質

Q 小時候，堆積木是很多人常玩的遊戲，假如現在再給你一堆積木，你會嘗試堆出一個什麼樣的建築物呢？

A：木屋

B：宮殿

C：城堡

D：四合院

測驗結果
請見下頁

辦公室篇

貿易篇

業務篇

行銷篇

感情篇

測驗結果

A：你是一個能忍別人所不能忍的人。你擁有寬大的心胸，可以包容許多事情，在職場上總是抱著以和為貴的態度。

B：你是一個心思敏銳的人。對於身邊的事物都能有良好的安排，凡事都在你的掌握之中，沒有什麼心機，但能夠把複雜的人事關係都處理得很好，如魚得水。

C：你是一個厲害的人際高手，觀察事物極其敏銳，還能看透人心，而且你很享受這一切。

D：你是一個胸無大志的好好先生。沒有什麼企圖心，雖然你對周圍的感應能力不差，但由於你凡事只抱持著一顆平常心，你最大的好處就是不容易得罪人，簡簡單單的。

心理知識補一補

隨遇而安

　　在對話當中，Siobhan 對於看展的行程安排、住宿頗有微詞，相比較之下，Jingle 的態度就算的上是**隨遇而安**。在英文當中，若要形容隨遇而安，則可以說是 "To reconcile oneself to a challenging situation."。

　　有些人會認為隨遇而安是對於發生的事情採取不積極的態度。而在心理學的角度上分析，則認為這是人們適應社會的一種方式。而這種適應方式可分為積極適應及消極適應這兩種。

　　積極適應是像是 Jingle 在對話中表現出的，在面對臨時決定的膠囊旅館時，仍能以積極的態度，列舉出這一個住宿的優點來說服 Siobhan。這樣的態度往往能讓這類型的人在變化的環境當中取得優勢，或是支配的地位。而 Siobhan 則是屬於消極的適應，一般是順應著潮流變遷，在 Jingle 找到說服她的理由之後，便處於服從的地位。你是屬於那一種呢？

辦公室篇

貿易篇

業務篇

行銷篇

感情篇

Unit 6 業務會議

 前情提要

Roy, Ken, and Frank are in a sales meeting discussing their sales performance.

Roy、Ken 和 Frank 在一個業務會議裡面討論他們的銷售業績。

 角色介紹

Roy- The sales manager（業務經理）
Ken- A new Salesperson（一個新業務人員）
Frank- A senior salesperson（一個資深業務）

 情境對話

Roy: Good afternoon everyone. **Let me cut to the chase!** Our sales report indicates that our goals were not met and the revenue in the second quarter was 35% lower than usual. I do not allow it to happen again, and I want you to show me a growth in sales in the fourth quarter.

各位午安。讓我直接開門見山吧！我們的銷售報告指出我們未達標而且第二季的營收比去年同期下降了 35%。我不允許這再發生一次，而且我要你們在第四期給我看到營業額的成長。

Frank: Roy, please have a look at the sales report from last month, our sales

Roy 請看一下上個月的銷售報告，我們的銷售在一

業務會議 Unit 6

辦公室篇

貿易篇

業務篇

行銷篇

感情篇

increased by 5% just within a month. | 個月內就提升了 5%。

Roy: Not bad! Why is that? What sort of new strategy did you apply? | 不錯嘛！這是為什麼呢？你用了什麼新策略？

Frank: We hired Ken from our competitor. He is the legend! The top sales! | 我們從我們的對手那裡挖角了 Ken。他是傳奇！頂尖業務！

Roy: That is a good move! Ken, how did you manage to do that? | 這是很好的一步！Ken 你是怎麼做到的？

Ken: I brought some customers with me to the company, and I suggested us to enhance our after-sales services. **Simple as that!** | 我帶來了一些客戶到公司，然後我建議我們加強售後服務。就這麼簡單！

Roy: Alright, Frank you have to watch your back. Ken is coming after you!
The next sales meeting, I will not be here. I want Frank to be the chair. Our new business partner will be there too, be prepared and impress them. | 好，Frank 你要小心。Ken 是衝著你來的！
下一個業務會議我不會在這，我要 Frank 擔任主席。我們新的生意夥伴也會到，準備好然後讓他們刮目相看。

Frank: Okay, thanks for trusting me. | 好，謝謝你信任我。

Part 3

 前情提要

Ken and Frank are doing meeting preparation discussions before the next sales meeting.

Ken 和 Frank 正在做下一個業務會議之前的會前準備討論。

 角色介紹

Ken- A new salesperson（一個新業務人員）
Frank- A senior salesperson（一個資深業務）

 情境對話

Frank: The next sales meeting is in 2 weeks, and since our new business partner will be present as well, **we need to get our ducks in a row.**

下一個業務會議就在 2 個禮拜後了，因為我們的新生意夥伴也會出席，我們需要井井有條。

Ken: What do you want me to do?

你想要我怎麼做呢？

Frank: Please discuss the meeting agenda with the secretary, and I need you to provide a diagram of the revenue of the third quarter.

請和秘書討論議程，然後我需要你提供一個第三季銷售額的圖表。

Ken: Okay. What else?

好的。還有什麼？

Frank: If you can, I would like you to think of another proposal to bring our sales to the next level.

如果你可以，我想要你想另一個提案，讓我們的業績更上一層樓。

Ken: I am running out of ideas, but I will talk to the Marketing Department to see if they can assist us. I cannot promise though.

我沒有想法了，但我會和行銷部門討論看看他們是否可以協助我們。不過我不能保證。

Frank: Do your best.

你盡力就好。

Ken: By the way, I know our competitors have been trying hard to look for new investors. I suggest us find a new investor ahead them, then in the next meeting we can also show our new business partner that we are a stronger group.

對了，我知道我們的對手最近在努力找新投資商。我建議我們可以在他們之前找到新投資者，這樣在下個業務會議的時候，我們可以讓我們的新生意夥伴知道，我們是更強大的集團了。

Frank: Good point. Go run with it!

說的好。去做吧！

Part 3

辦公室心情隨筆

Frank:

Roy is not happy about the last quarter's sales. Luckily, I come prepared. Let me show him our incredible sales performance from last month, and I bet he will be pleased. It was smart of me to decide to hire Ken. Ken really saved us. I know Ken is good, but I did not know he is that good. No wonder he gets to be the legend.

Roy 對上一季的業績不滿意。幸好我有備而來。讓我給他看我們上個月驚人的銷售業績，我保證他會高興。雇用 Ken 我真是聰明。Ken 真的救了我們。Ken 好，但是我不知道他那麼好。難怪他可以成為傳奇。

Roy is right, and I need to watch out, or soon Ken will take over my job. However, I am not that worried, as I know Roy will not do that to me, as long as I keep my sales steady. See! Roy trusts me that much to let me be the chair for the next sales meeting. This means huge to me.

Roy 是對的，我需要小心，不然很快的 Ken 會搶走我的工作。然而，我沒有那麼擔心，因為我知道只要我保持銷售平穩的話，Roy 不會那樣對我。看吧！Roy 那麼相信我，讓我當下次業務會議的主席。這對我而言意義深大。

Okay, now I need to call Ken for some discussions, we need to do some preparations for the next sales meeting, and I cannot do it without Ken. I will just tell him what I need him to do. He is so cool that he can always bring me something unexpected. Our next sales meeting is now looking good. I totally have nothing to worry about and be afraid of.

好，現在我要叫 Ken 來做些討論，我們需要為下次的業務會議做一些會議準備，而沒有 Ken 我做不來。我告訴他我需要他做什麼就好了。

184

他好酷他總是能給我帶來一些意想不到的。我們的下一個業務會議看起來不錯。我完全沒有需要擔心和害怕的。

 Ken:

Roy is not satisfied with the sales from the last quarter. I know Frank has a copy of last month's sale with him now. He said he will show it to Roy when necessary. I think now is the time for it.

Roy 對於上一季的業績不滿意。我知道 Frank 現在有一份上個月的銷售報表。他說必要的時候他會秀給 Roy 看。我想現在就是那個時機了。

Good, it works! Roy seems surprised for the sales performance.

很好，成功了！Roy 看起來對於這個業績表現很訝異。

Now Frank is finally introducing me to Roy. Roy just asked Frank to watch his back, is he implying something here? Does he think that I want to take Frank's position? Maybe not, I am just being paranoid I think. He is asking Frank to be the chair of the next sales meeting, looks like he trusts Frank a lot, and he thinks Frank has the ability to manage the meeting well. If he does not have enough confidence in Frank, then he will not miss the next meeting as our new business partner will be there, too.

現在 Frank 終於要向 Roy 介紹我了。Roy 剛叫 Frank 要小心，他是在暗指什麼嗎？他以為我想要奪走 Frank 的位置嗎？也許不是，我想只是我在多疑。他要 Frank 當下一個業務會議的主席，看來他很相信 Frank，而且他認為 Frank 有能力主持好這會議。如果他對 Frank 沒有足夠的信心，那他就不會錯過下次會議了，因為我們的新生意夥伴也會

辦公室篇

貿易篇

業務篇

行銷篇

感情篇

去。

Okay, I guess it's time for the meeting preparation. He is in charge, so I will just follow his orders. All he is asking me to do are basic things. How about me telling him the news I just heard, and let him know what I am up to.

好，我想是時候作會議準備了。他主導所以我就遵從命令就好了。他叫我做的所有都是基本的。不如我告訴他我剛聽到的消息，然後讓他知道我想怎麼做。

 ## 好好用句型

★ **Let me cut to the chase!**

讓我直接開門見山吧！

cut to the chase

開門見山／有話直說

> Or you can say:
> - get to the point
>   有話直說
> - get this straight
>   開門見山；直接說

★ **Simple as that!**

就這麼簡單！

> Or you can say:
> - That's all there is to it.
>   就這麼簡單。
> - It is that simple / That's it!
>   就是這麼簡單。／就這樣。

★ **We need to get our ducks in a row.**
我們需要井井有條。

ducks in a row 井井有條

Or you can say:

- in a good order
  整整齊齊
- in apple-pie order
  有條不紊、井然有序

 心理小測試

企圖心

Q 每個人在童年時，大多都有個娃娃。其實，從你喜歡的娃娃類型，就能看出你的企圖心的。現在請你回想一下，你最愛哪一種類型的娃娃呢？

A：布娃娃

B：塑膠人形娃娃

C：填充娃娃

D：木頭娃娃

測驗結果
請見下頁

辦公室篇

貿易篇

業務篇

行銷篇

感情篇

187

測 驗 結 果

A：你的企圖心指數為 **30%**。其實你沒什麼企圖心，你不僅害怕失敗，也害怕成功所相對要面臨的責任感，所以在處事上總是患得患失，無法全力向目標衝刺。

B：你的企圖心指數為 **95%**。你的企圖心非常強，讓人很難忽視你的存在，但你卻無法真正的確定自己的目標，只為追求金錢何名利的你，好像是為了別的人眼光而活著一樣。

C：你的企圖心指數為 **80%**。你的企圖心是彈性的，容易為了不想被比下去而死拼，但是一旦沒有了比較的對象，你就失去了鬥志。

D：你的企圖心指數為 **65%**。你不是沒有企圖心，只是你追求的不是別人眼中所謂的成就。你知道自己要的是什麼，所以你在追求的過程中，是不管世俗眼光，自己享受樂趣的。

心理知識補一補

鯰魚效應

　　相信大家都同意如果要吃海鮮，最好是吃新鮮的，除了安全上的考量之外，還有新鮮的海鮮肉質也比較好吃，味道也更加地鮮美。據說在 19 世紀初的挪威，沿岸突然出現了大量的沙丁魚，而隨著有一名法國人在挪威建立了一個當時全歐洲最大的沙丁魚罐頭工廠，許多挪威人則是以沙丁魚的相關產業為生。而死掉的沙丁魚及活跳跳的沙丁魚在價格上有極大的差異，而當時卻只有一位船長將捕到的沙丁魚活生生的送上岸販售。後來發現這個船長的秘方是將一條沙丁魚的天敵鯰魚放在魚獲的容器中，沙丁魚為了躲避鯰魚，就會奮力地在容器中游動，也因此增加了存活的機會。而這就是我要談的「鯰魚效應」（**Catfish Effect**）的由來。

　　後來在管理心理學上利用這樣的理論在職場中安排一個新進的競爭者，往往能夠激勵整個團隊的士氣。也正如在對話當中，Frank 雇用了能力強的 Ken，而 Ken 的優異表現，在上司 Roy 的提醒下讓 Frank 因此有了危機意識，但也在 Roy 適時的交付給 Frank 更重要的任務，化解了Frank 心中對 Ken 的一些疑慮，也能因此而期待這個團隊之間會有更加的良性競爭表現。

Part 4
行銷篇

Part 4

Unit 1 秘密客就在你身邊

 前情提要

Blake is telling Serena about a rumor she heard.

Blake 正在告訴 Serena 關於她聽到的傳言。

 角色介紹

Blake- Sales 1 （業務 1）
Serena- Sales 2 （業務 2）
Dan- Sales 3 （業務 3）

 情境對話

Blake: Serena, I heard a rumor says that the board recently hired a mystery shopper.

Serena，我聽到一個傳聞說，董事會最近雇用了一位神秘客。

Serena: Are you sure? What is the point of doing that?

你肯定嗎？這樣做的目的是什麼？

Blake: They just want to evaluate our performance in a new way, I guess.

我想他們只是想以一個新的方式評估我們的表現吧。

Dan: Serena, you have nothing to worry. You are the best sales here with the best service too. **I am glad that today is my last day though, so I can stay out of it.**

Serena，妳不用擔心啊，妳是這裡最棒的業務也有最好的服務。我很高興今天是我的最後一天，我就可以置身事外了。

Blake: Dan, **stop apple-polishing her!**

Dan 停止拍她馬屁！

Serena: We are all professionally-trained; therefore, a mystery shopper is not a big deal.

我們都是受過專業訓練的，所以一個神秘客沒有什麼大不了的。

Blake: I know. I just do not feel comfortable with it. It is like a surveillance which is alive and we do not know it existed.

我知道，我只是對此覺得不舒服，就好像是一個活生生的監視器，而我們不知道它的存在。

Serena: Well, **with things as such, we will have to let it slide.**

這個嘛，事已至此，我們只能順其自然了。

Blake: I just cannot accept it, I hope the mystery shopper goes to you, not me.

我就是不能接受，我希望那個神秘客去找你，不是我。

Serena: It is okay with me.

對我來說可以啊。

Part 4

 前情提要

Blake is telling Serena about a complaint she got from a customer.
Blake 在告訴 Serena 關於一個她得到的投訴。

 角色介紹

Blake- Sales 1 （業務 1）
Serena- Sales 2 （業務 2）

 情境對話

Blake: Guess what? There was a complaint about me, and it was sent directly to the board.	你知道嗎？有個對我的投訴，然後直接送到董事會去了。
Serena: It is the girl from last week, am I right? You did not take out your professional side. I saw it.	是上禮拜那個女的，我說的對嗎？妳沒有拿出妳專業的一面。我有看到。
Blake: Yes. Though that was because she was asking too many questions, and took me the whole afternoon and she did not sign any car.	對。可是那是因為她問太多問題了，而且她花了我一整個下午還沒簽半輛車。
Serena: Customers are supposed to have a lot of questions. That is why we have to recite all those answers from the list of questions, remember? We are trained to be patient. This is our job.	客戶本該就有很多問題的。這就是為什麼我們要背那麼多問題清單上面答案，記得嗎？ 我們被訓練成要有耐心，這是我們的工作。

Blake: I know that now. I still have a lot to learn I admit. Sometimes, when you face the real situation, it is hard to do what the tutorial tells you.

我現在知道了，我還有很多要學，我承認。有時候當妳遇到真實狀況的時候，很難去做教程教妳的。

Serena: Just how that complaint went directly to the board not to our manager first?

那個投訴是怎麼直接到董事會而不是先到我們主管手上的？

Blake: That was the mystery shopper. That is why.

那就是那位神秘客，這就是為什麼。

Serena: Murphy's Law!

莫非定律！

辦公室篇

貿易篇

業務篇

行銷篇

感情篇

195

Part 4

辦公室心情隨筆

Blake:

What? They say the board of our company just hired a mystery shopper to test us? I must go tell Serena about this. Serena does not get why they are doing it. People do not just hire a mystery shopper out of nothing. It is a test to us. Dan is such a real bootlicker! Although he is right about Serena, he still sounds disgusting. Dan is lucky because he does not have to be evaluated through this way. Serena is so okay with it. I do not like the idea at all. I do not want to be watched unknown. If that is acceptable with Serena, and she is that confident, please let the mystery shopper choose Serena. I am so weak with tough customers.

什麼？他們說我們公司的董事會雇用了一個神秘客來測試我們？我必須去告訴 Serena 這件事。Serena 不懂她們為什麼這樣做。人們才不會沒事就請一個神秘客，是對我們的測試。Dan 真是個馬屁精！雖然他說 Serena 說的對，聽起來還是噁心。Dan 好幸運可以不用這樣被測試。Serena 覺得好，沒問題。我一點都不喜歡這種做法，我不想在未知的情況下被監控。如果 Serena 覺得這可以接受也這麼有自信，請讓神秘客去選擇 Serena 吧。我對於難搞的客人很弱。

What? I got a complaint? A customer from last week? It's got to be that girl, as that was the only deal I did not make and I was not patient with her I know. What? She is the mystery shopper? How lucky I am! I wish she did not come to me! I am going to tell Serena about this. Serena is right about me. It is actually my fault to be complained.

什麼？我得到一個投訴？上禮拜的客人？一定是那女的，因為那是我唯一沒達成的交易，而且我知道我對她沒耐心。什麼？她就是秘密客？我多幸運啊！我真希望她沒來找我！我要告訴 Serena 這件事。Serena 說我說的對，我被抱怨事實上是我的錯。

Serena:

What? A mystery shopper? What for? Is that really necessary? If they want to see our sales performance, they can just read the numbers from the sales report. Dan is correct I have nothing to worry, I am always professional with each customer. Dan is really lucky though, as who would want to be evaluated this way. However, it is really not that big deal. I think Blake is over-reacting. Whether she can accept it or not, it is happening anyway.

什麼？一個神秘客？為什麼？那樣是真的有必要的嗎？如果他們想看我們的業績表現，他們可以直接看銷售報告上的數字就好了。Dan 是正確的，我沒什麼好擔心的，我對每個客人總是很專業的。Dan 是真的很幸運就是了，因為沒有人會想要被這樣評估。然而，這真的不是什麼大不了的。我覺得 Blake 有些過度反應了。不管她可不可以接受，都是要發生的。

What? Blake was complained and the complaint was sent directly to the board? That is really bad, this will look bad in her file. That should be from the girl last week, but she got that coming. She was not professional with her. She should not have any excuses to a bad service. She is not new, she should not still be making this kind of mistake. She should be patient with each customer like what we were taught to and told to. How come that girl's complaint could go directly to the board? I thought our manager should get it first. That was the mystery shopper? She was so real though! This is really the Murphy's law!

什麼？Blake 被投訴了而且那個投訴直接到了董事會那邊？真是不好，這在她檔案上看起來會不好。這應該是上禮拜那個女的，但是那是她自找的，她對她很不專業。對於不好的服務她不應該有任何藉口。她不是新人了，她不該還犯這種錯誤。她對每位客人都應該有耐心，就如同我們所被教導的及被告知的。為什麼那女士的抱怨可以直接到董事會去？我以為我們的主管會先拿到。那就是神秘客嗎？但是她好真實！這真的是莫非定律！

 好好用句型

★ **I am glad that today is my last day though, so I can stay out of it.**

我很高興今天是我的最後一天，我就可以置身事外了。

stay out of it

置身事外

　　Or you can say:

- sit on the sidelines

袖手旁觀（有置身事外之意）

- stay aloof from the affair

置身事外

★ **Stop apple-polishing her!**

停止拍她馬屁！

apple-polishing sb.

拍……馬屁

　　Or you can say:

- butter her up

對她阿諛奉承

- kiss her ass
  拍她馬屁

★ **With things as such, we will have to let it slide.**
事到如今,我們也只好順其自然了。

Let it slide.
順其自然。

    Or you can say:
- Leave it up to the destiny
  看緣分吧。
- Leave it as it is
  順其自然。

心理小測試

你是職場黑馬嗎?

Q 假如有一天你被外星人抓走了,你接下來會怎麼做呢?

A:想辦法找機會逃走
B:裝死或者假裝睡著
C:求外星人放走自己

測驗結果
請見下頁

辦公室篇

貿易篇

業務篇

行銷篇

感情篇

測驗結果

A：你有明日之星的架式，有機會成為天王天后的接班人。你對自己很有自信，平常會在專業上投資自己，只要有任何學習的機會就會很努力去學，因此等到時機出現時，就會令人刮目相看。

B：你目前已經是職場紅人，已經得到上司的看重，也會被委以重任。你除了自己本身的努力以外，也是位 EQ 非常高的人，你懂得包容與分享，即使自己已經是紅人，也還是會和大家分享你的光環。所以你不僅事業有成，人也很沉穩。

C：你是屬於默默奉獻的人，不過你的努力總有一天會被看到的。你只求默默耕耘卻不求被大家注意，你認為只要做好自己份內的事就好了，你認為只要自己腳踏實地往前走，一步一腳印的總有一天一定會成功。

 知識補一補

莫非定律 Murphy's Law

"Who's Murphy?" 『誰是莫非？』

「莫非」其實是美國愛德華茲空軍基地的一位上尉工程師，名叫 Ed Murphy，在 1949 年時找出了當時的火箭減速超重試驗的失敗原因是因為儀表被裝反了，而在當時的一封信中提到 "That law's namesake was Capt. Ed Murphy… 'If there is any way to do it wrong, and he will'…"（這個定律的同名名稱為 Ed Murphy 上尉……，"如果有被做錯的方法的話，那他就會這樣做"……）這裡的他指的是裝反儀表的技術人員。

莫非定律被稱為是在 20 世紀西方文化中的三大發現之一，但其實自古即有這樣類似的說法－「麵包落地時，總是塗有奶油的那一面著地。」而莫非定律則是 "Anything that can go wrong will go wrong."（凡有可能出錯的事都會出錯。）後來被廣泛的利用在人及工業管理上。對於所有的事有最壞的預測，及因應這種最糟糕的情況來做最完善的準備。例如是在游泳池也放置有滅火器材，以及為了防止人為因素及許多可預知的狀況而設計的「防呆」（Fool Proofing）裝置。

辦公室篇

貿易篇

業務篇

行銷篇

感情篇

Unit 2 行銷策略

 前情提要

Blair is giving Chuck a case in the office.

Blair 在辦公室裡給 Chuck 一個案子。

 角色介紹

Blair- Marketing manager（行銷經理）

Chuck- The account planner（客戶策劃人員）

 情境對話

Blair: Chuck, we have a new case here I want you to take over. This client here, the other companies went to them before us, but their marketing strategies did not interest them.

Chuck，我們這裡有個新案子，我要你接手。這個客戶，在我們之前，有其他公司去過，但是他們的行銷策略沒有引起他們的興趣。

Chuck: I think we need to do a lot of marketing researches for this case. I will conduct both online and offline surveys to basically find out who the target audiences should be, and then we will go from there.

我想這個案子我們需要做很多的市場調查，我會進行線上和線下的問卷，基本上要找出他們的目標客戶應該是誰，然後從邊繼續。

Blair: The product failed, you will first of all figure out why the product failed.

這產品已經失敗了,你首先要釐清為什麼這個產品會失敗。

Chuck: Okay, I will liaise with the client to identify specific product problems.

好,我會和客戶聯絡,確定具體的產品問題。

Blair: **They sort of have their back up against the wall now**. Basically, they are looking for a right marketing strategy to the right people at the right place and at the right time, and those answers are for us to give them.

他們現在有點無能為力了,基本上,他們在找的是在對的時間和對的地點給對的人一個對的行銷策略,而這些答案是要由我們給他們。

Chuck: Noted. I will have all the data collected and analyzed and come up with a marketing strategy that they could not resist by next week.

知道了。我會在下週前把所有資料收集分析好,然後想出一個他們無法抵抗的行銷策略。

Blair: Do not come back empty-handed; I **want you to come back with your arms full.**

別空手而回,我要你滿載而歸。

Part 4

 前情提要

Blair is asking Chuck to give her the marketing strategy that she asked for.
Blair 在要求 Chuck 給她她要求的行銷策略。

 角色介紹

Blair- Marketing manager（行銷經理）
Chuck- The account planner（客戶策劃人員）

 情境對話

Blair: Chuck, tell me you have something for me!

Chuck，告訴我你有東西要給我了！

Chuck: I am so sorry, but I still need more time.

我很抱歉，但是我還需要更多時間。

Blair: Are you not aware that the deadline is in two days?
If you require more time, you should have said so! Now is too late for that.

你知道截止日期是兩天後嗎？
如果你需要更多時間！你就應該要說了！現在太遲了。

Chuck: **Fine products come from slow work.**
Just ask them to give us one more week; it will be worth it. I promise.

慢工出細活。

只是要求他們多給我們一個禮拜，我保證會是值得的。

You know I can give you whatever

妳知道我現在這秒就可以

strategy right this second, but even you will not buy it. We are just doing some more researches to support our idea.

給妳個隨便的策略，但是連妳都不會被說服。我們只是在做更多的調查來支持我們的想法。

Blair: Okay I will do that. I will buy you some more time.
I am only doing that for you because I know you have never disappointed me.

好吧，我會那樣做，我會幫你爭取更多時間。
我會為你這樣做只是因為我知道你從未讓我失望過。

Please do not prove me wrong this time.

這次請不要證明我錯了。

Chuck: I will not let you down, and I will not let this customer walk away.

我不會讓妳失望，也不會讓客戶走掉。

Part 4

辦公室心情隨筆

Blair:

Here is a case that looks impossible to fix. However, I know just who to give it to. Chuck can salvage the situation easily like always. Now I will call him and simply explain the situation to him, he will do the rest himself. Chucks can always find a solution to a problem and he always knows what to do. Now he wants to focus on the target audience, but it is not just that. It is not that simple, let me just remind him a bit. Now he is getting more serious about this case, I hope he can give me some good news next week.

這裡有個案子看起來很難救。然而，我知道就該給誰。Chuck 可以如往常一樣很輕鬆挽回局面。現在我要叫他，然後簡單跟他解釋狀況，他就會自己做剩下的了。Chuck 總是可以替問題找到答案然後總是知道該怎麼做。現在他說要專注在目標客戶，但是不是只是那樣，沒有那麼簡單，讓我稍微提醒他一下。現在他對這個案子更認真了，我希望下禮拜他可以給我一些好消息。

Okay, now is almost the deadline. Let me follow up with Chuck, see if he has finished his researches and if he got a marketing strategy for this client. I cannot wait to hear it out! What? No results yet? We promised to give the client something in 2 days. Now he is saying that he does not have the marketing strategy for them yet? Okay, if Chuck needs more time, he must got his own reason to it. I have to trust him and request more time for him.

好，現在已經快到期限了，讓我跟 Chuck 跟進一下看他是不是完成他的調查，以及是否有一個給客戶的行銷策略了。我等不及聽到了！什麼？還沒有結果？我們承諾在 2 天後要給這個客戶一些東西的。現在他說他還沒有給他們的行銷策略？好吧，如果 Chuck 需要更多時間，他必定有他的理由。我必須信任他還有幫他要求更多時間。

 Chuck:

Blair is giving me a case? I always get the tough ones from her. It is always the same, some good researches will lead us to the right path. I will firstly discover the client's target audience. It looks like it is not just about who to target. Also, the product itself might be wrong somehow, I will get in touch with the client and see if I can figure anything. Blair is right, all those elements need to be right. I think I might need more detailed researches than the other cases, I should have all the data back and analyzed before next week. I cannot wait to see some answers through the results.

Blair 要給我一個案子？我總是從她那拿到艱難的。總是一樣的，一些好的調查就會帶領我們到正確的道路上。我會首先找出客人的目標客戶。看來不是只是關於要瞄準誰，還有產品本身不知怎麼的可能有問題，我會跟客戶聯絡上，看我能不能找出任何。Blair 是對的，那些因素都要是對的。我想比起其他案子我需要更多的調查，我應該可以在下禮拜之前拿回所有數據以及分析完。我等不及透過結果看答案了。

Oh no. Blair is now asking me to give her the marketing strategy, which I do not have the right one for the client yet. I will just be honest and tell her I need more time then.

Thanks Blair for having my back and trusting me. I can do better with her trust. I will not let her down and I will not let us lose this client. I will let our strategy speaks for itself.

噢不。Blair 現在要求我給她行銷策略，我還沒有合適的可以給客戶。我就誠實告訴她我需要更多時間好了。謝謝 Blair 支持我和信任我。有她的信任我可以做得更好。我不會讓她失望也不會讓我們失去這個客戶。我會讓我們的策略自己會說話。

 好好用句型

★ **They sort of have their back up against the wall now.**
他們現在有點無能為力了。

back up against the wall
無能為力

　　Or you can say:

- There is nothing I can do.
　我也沒辦法了。（有無力感。）
- This is out of my hands.
　此事已非我能力所及。

★ **I want you to come back with your arms full.**
我要你滿載而歸。

come back With arms full 滿載而歸

　　Or you can say:

- Return home with pockets full.
　口袋滿滿的回家。（即為滿載而歸之意）
- Return with fruitful results.
　帶著豐碩的成果回來。（亦為滿載而歸）

★ **Fine products come from slow work.**
慢工出細活。

　　Or you can say:

- You cannot rush the best.
　最好的事是急不得的。（慢工出細活）

- Rome was not built in a day.
  羅馬不是一天造成的。（即慢工出細活之意）

 **心理小測試**

失敗後的你

Q 在幼稚園裡面或幼兒時期，你最喜歡玩的遊戲是以下哪個呢？

A：盪鞦韆

B：翹翹板

C：爬竿

D：溜滑梯

測驗結果
請見下頁

辦公室篇

貿易篇

業務篇

行銷篇

感情篇

測驗結果

A：孝順的你因為怕家人擔心，所以會努力讓自己站起來。你心腸很軟，而且很容易牽掛父母家人，對你而言，家永遠是最溫暖的避風港，有家人的鼓勵才站得起來。在工作上如果跌倒了，你的第一個想法就是不能讓家人擔心。

B：你有運動家精神，會反省失敗原因後再站起來。你應變能力強，能夠掌握自己的平衡點，失敗時的第一個直覺就是要先冷靜下來，先反省問題出在哪裡，之後再參考別人的意見重新出發。

C：你不服輸的個性會讓你逼自己在最短的時間站起來。你的自尊心比你的應變能力還要強，因為你是個不輕易認輸的人。就算你狀態再不好，你也會逼自己馬上爬起來。

D：當失敗後，你首先想到的是找個地方尋求解脫，或是想先流浪一陣子再找新機會。你很信任別人，如果你失敗了通常就是對信任的人失去信心了，或是被信任的人出賣而失敗，此時的你會對人性有不信任感或是疏離感，因此會自己放空沉澱一下再出發。

心理知識補一補

崔西定律

　　如何有效的管理時間，對於每一個上班族都相當的重要。這裡要談的崔西定律（Tracy's Law）則是針對管理階層提出建議要如何提高部屬的工作效率，以節省大量的時間。

　　其實這一個方法相當的簡單，就是簡化工作上的流程。崔西定律指出「任何工作的困難度與其執行步驟的數目平方成正比：例如完成一件工作有 3 個執行步驟，則此工作的困難度是 9，而完成另一工作有 5 個執行步驟，則此工作的困難度是 25，所以必須要簡化工作流程。」簡化工作流程除了能節省工作時間，提高工作效率之外，也能有效地降低錯誤。管理學者認為，能有效地簡化工作流程是大多數成功主管的共同特質。

　　在對話中，如果 Blair 與 Chuck 在執行這一個項目之前能先就工作流程上來討論，由 Blair 來簡化工作步驟，也許 Chuck 就能在時間內完成。但事情已經發生，與其追問部屬要如何解決，還不如做個有擔當的主管，為了有更好的工作成效，主動承擔責任，向客戶爭取更多的時間。

辦公室篇

貿易篇

業務篇

行銷篇

感情篇

Unit 3 廣告一手包

 前情提要

Meredith is in Dereck's office trying to understand the way Dereck's service works.

Meredith 在 Dereck 的辦公室裡試圖了解 Dereck 的服務的運作方式。

 角色介紹

Dereck- The account manager（客戶經理）
Meredith- The client（客戶）

 情境對話

Meredith: Hi, we are launching a new product and we need experts in advertising.
Tell me why coming to you will have better results than doing it by ourselves?

你好，我們要推出一個新產品，我們需要廣告方面的專家。
告訴我為什麼找你們的結果會比我們自己做還要好呢？

Dereck: **We have been providing end to end advertising service for years**. We know our roles and we know how to package a product in the market.

我們已經提供一條龍的廣告服務多年了，我們知道我們的角色，也知道怎麼在市場上包裝一個產品。

Meredith: Assuming we decide to work with you, how does it work? How do we proceed? We already have a rough business plan by the way.

假使我們決定和你們合作了，這是如何運作的？我們要怎麼進行？我們已經有個概略的商業計畫了。

Dereck: **First of all**, we will come up with a marketing strategy and the creative brief based on your business plan. The next will be the media planning stage where you can pick your own preferred media channel. Then we move on to the advertising development stage. Lastly, we will have the whole package back to you for you to start the production or take actions.

首先，我們根據妳的商業計畫提出一個行銷策略和創意簡報，再來就是媒體規劃階段，這裡妳可以選擇你自己偏好的媒體頻道，然後前進到廣告開發階段，最後我們會把整套歸還給你讓你們開始做生產或者採取動作。

We will have your authorization at each stage before we move forward, so at the end, you will get exactly what you want.

我們在每一個階段，會得到妳的授權才向前，所以最後妳會得到你們確切要的。

Meredith: That sounds like a perfect plan, but the cost is a bit high though.

那聽起來是個完美的計劃，但是花費有點高就是了。

Dereck: **You get what you pay for**.

一分錢一分貨。

Meredith: Okay, let us get started.

好，讓我們開始吧。

Part 4

前情提要

Meredith is now in Dereck's office discussing their promotional plan.

Meredith 現在在 Dereck 的辦公室裡面討論他們的促銷計畫。

角色介紹

Dereck- The account manager（客戶經理）
Meredith- The client（客戶）

情境對話

Meredith: So far we are very satisfied with your team's work. We love the advertising plan at this stage; however, it is the promotional plan we would like to discuss further with you in person.

到目前為止我們非常滿意你們團隊的工作。我們喜歡現階段的廣告計劃，但是是促銷計畫我們想親自做進一步的討論。

Dereck: Sure, since it is soon for releasing this new product of yours.
Now let us go over the promotional plan together.

當然，因為很快就到妳們新產品的發表了。
現在讓我們來一起看看這促銷計畫吧。

Meredith: Like you suggested. We will do the free sample tasting for the first week of launching that is a good idea. How about the print and radio?

如你所建議的。我們在上市的第一個禮拜做免費試吃是個好主意。那麼平面和廣播呢？

Dereck: We have covered that. We have put you all over the radio and relevant

我們已經有進行了，我們把你們放置在各大廣播和

magazines, but we are also recommending social media.

相關雜誌裡，但我們也推薦你們利用社群媒體。

Meredith: Okay, we will start by creating its Facebook page.

好，我們會開始建立商品的臉書專頁。

Dereck: You will need to interact with your customers often, put latest updates and all that.

你們需要常跟客戶互動，放上最新資訊那些的。

Meredith: Okay, we will do that. So that is it? Is the product finally ready to go now?

好，我們會這麼做。所以就這樣了嗎？現在產品終於可以上市了嗎？

Dereck: Yes, it is the time!

是的，時候到了！

Part 4

 辦公室心情隨筆

 Meredith:

Now we have a product ready to launch, but how is it going out there in the market? We do not want to take any risks. We should go seek for someone professional. I know there is a team for this, and they cover everything for you.

現在我們有準備好要上市的產品了，但是要怎麼到市場上呢？我們不想冒任何險。我們應該去問專業的人。我知道有個團隊做這個的，而且他們包辦所有事情。

Okay, here I am in their office. Let me tell him what we want and see if he can convince me for working with them or not. Okay, he has got his point. How does all this work then? That whole plan is very detailed and really do all the works for you. This can save us a lot of time and it can save us from making mistakes. He is right; we should be getting what we pay for at the end. Okay, deal!

好，我們現在在他們的辦公室了，讓我告訴他我們要什麼然後看他能不能說服我和他們合作。好，他有他的說法。那麼這一切要怎麼運作呢？整個計畫很詳細而且真的幫你做所有工作，這樣可以省很多時間還有避免我們犯錯。他是對的，我們最後應該會得到我們所付出的。好吧，成交！

Now all other parts are done and we are happy about that. Let me discuss the promotional plan with them as we need to know more details about how our product is going to be known. Okay, now even the promotional sounds perfect. We will do all they suggested, too. It is so good to know that our product is finally launching.

現在所有其它部分都好了，而我們很滿意。讓我來跟他們討論促銷計畫，因為我們需要知道更多我們的產品要怎麼被知道的細節。好，現在連促銷計劃聽起來都完美了。我們也會做他們建議的。知道我們的產品終於要上市了真是太好了。

Dereck:

Okay, a new client coming in. Of course we can do better in adverting; otherwise, why did we establish this company for? We know how to dress your product up, that is it.

好，一個新客戶走進來了。當然我們在廣告上可以做得比較好，否則我們成立這家公司做什麼？我們知道怎麼幫你的產品打扮，就是這樣。

Okay, she is not familiar with the process, let me explain each step to her and let her understand that they still have a say in each stage. Basically, they still take control at each phase. Without their authorization, it will make things harder to move on.

好，她對過程不太熟悉，讓我跟她解釋每一個步驟，然後讓她知道他們在每一個階段都有權表達意見，基本上在每個階段他們仍有控制權。沒有他們授權，只會讓事情更難進行。

Now she is suggesting that the cost is too high. Please do not start bargaining. We will not lower the cost. Okay, finally we got this case now.

現在她覺得我們價錢太高了。拜託別開始討價還價，我們不會降價的。好，我們終於得到這個案子了。

Okay, now they are asking for another meeting, what might that for? Oh, they love the advertising plan, but they want more details on the promotional plan. Of course, they are starting to get nervous as they are launching their new product *soon.*

好，現在他們在要求另一個會議，會是為了什麼呢？噢，他們愛這個廣告計劃，但是他們要促銷計畫的細節。他們當然會緊張，因為他們快要上市新產品了。

Now I will talk through the whole promotional plan, so we know where to add or edit. Yes, free sample tasting is crucial for the very first week. The print and radio are organized in no doubt. Now I just need them to create and run any social media.

現在我會跟她講整個促銷計劃，我們就可以知道哪裡要增加或編輯。是的，在產品上市的第一週有免費試吃是很重要的。平面和廣播不用懷疑的當然有安排好。現在我只需要他們創造和經營任何社群媒體。

好好用句型

★ **We have been providing end to end advertising service for years.**

我們已經提供一條龍的廣告服務多年了。

end to end service

一條龍服務

Or you can say:

- all-in-one service

  整合全方位服務

- the whole package

  全包（有一條龍之意）

★ **First of all, …**

首先，……

Or you can say:

- to begin with
  由……開始
- above all
  首要的是

★ **You get what you pay for.**
  一分錢一分貨。

　　Or you can say:

- Every extra penny deserves its value.
  每分錢都有每分錢的價值。（即有一分錢一分貨之意）
- It is worth every penny of it.
  每分錢都是值得的。（即有一分錢一分貨之意）

心理小測試

創意

Q 你最常選用的雨傘的花色，是以下哪一種呢？

　　A：有大圖案的傘面

　　B：有零碎小圖案的傘面

　　C：格子面的傘面

　　D：單一素色的傘面

測驗結果
請見下頁

測 驗 結 果

A：你不是個很有創意的人，不過若是在工作上或是在生活上，如果遇到志同道合而且瞭解你的人，就能激發你的潛能，把你超乎想像的創意給逼出來。

B：你是個很有創造力的人，總是有很多鬼點子，不管是在工作上或者生活上總是有很多新的想法，也勇於提出並付諸行動，朋友或同事們也常佩服你新穎的想法。

C：你很有想像力，可是你的創造力卻因此有時令人難以理解，朋友或同事都摸不著頭緒，大家可能也不太能接受。

D：基本上你的創造力很少用於工作上，因為你覺得把創造力運用在生活上或娛樂上是比較有趣的，至於工作，你覺得你好好完成就好了。

心理知識補一補

◇◇ 交給專業人士

　　根據史丹福大學商學院的教授 Baba Shiv 所做的一項決策研究指出，「其實在有些時候將決定權交給別人也很不錯。」

　　在 Baba Shiv 的研究中，將受試者分成兩組，A 組可以選擇是要喝含有咖啡因的茶，亦或是有舒緩效果的洋甘菊茶，而 B 組的受試者沒有選擇，只能喝隨機選出的茶。在喝完茶的 5 分鐘後，受試者接受一項根據受試者程度來調整的謎題測試，一共有 15 道題，限時 30 分鐘。就理論上而言，一種是可以振奮精神、一個則是能舒緩緊張的茶，A 組的受試者有決定權以自身狀況選擇要的茶，所以測試結果應該較 B 組佳，但事實卻相反。A 組的平均答對題數為 5.8 題，而 B 組為 7.9 題。研究中指出人在做了選擇之後，往往會有要對自己的選擇負責，而有壓力，因此影響到答題時的情緒。

　　在職場當中亦然，對於很多事要做出選擇，與其事必躬親，還不如適當地放手，對於自己不熟悉的領域，就交給專業人士吧！**"Let the Pro do it!"**。

辦公室篇

貿易篇

業務篇

行銷篇

感情篇

Unit 4 公關大師

 前情提要

Christina is talking to Burke toward a public relations plan for their company.

Christina 正在和 Burke 談關於她們公司的公關計劃。

 角色介紹

Christina- The client（客戶）

Burke- The Public Relation that represent Christina's company（代表 Christina 公司的公關）

 情境對話

Christina: Burke, we need you for our company. We hope to create and maintain a positive relationship between our company and the community. Moreover, we need you to speak for us for any crisis.

Burke 我們公司需要你，我們希望建立與維持我們公司與社會大眾的良好關係。再來，我們需要你在任何危機時幫我們發聲。

Burke: I know what my role is. Although I do speaking for living, **I will not talk more than I perform.**

I see myself very professional and am

我知道我的角色是什麼。雖然我靠說話為生，但我不會光說不做的。

我認為自己很專業，也很

responsible for managing each company's business reputation.
If you think I am not good at damage controls, **you have no idea!**

替每家公司負責其商譽。如果妳認為我不擅於危機處理，那妳大錯特錯了！

Christina: You are just the right person for our company. However, can you explain to me how a public relations agency differs from an advertising agency? Sometimes I got this two confused.

你就是適合我們公司的人。但是，你可以跟我解釋一下一家廣告公司跟一家公關公司有何不同嗎？有時候我會把兩個搞混。

Burke: **In short, they do** "**paid media**" **and we do** "**free media**" **and** "**earned media**" , they pay for put up advertisements. We write or tell story and earn trusts and credibility.

簡單來說，他們做的是「付費的媒體」，而我們做的是「免費的媒體」以及「賺來的媒體」，他們付錢放廣告，我們寫故事或說故事來贏得信任和可信度。

Christina: Okay, then can you start representing us by holding a press conference next Friday? Later, we will sign a non-disclosure agreement first.

好的，那麼你可以從下週五舉行的一個記者發表會開始代表我們公司嗎？等等我們會先簽一個保密協議。

Burke: Yes to both.

兩者都好。

Part 4

 前情提要

Christina is discussing with Burke about a press conference tomorrow.

Christina 在跟 Burke 討論一個明天的記者會。

 角色介紹

Christina: The client（客戶）

Burke: The Public Relation that represents Christina's company（代表 Christina 公司的公關）

 情境對話

Christina: Have you booked us the place for the press conference yet?	你有幫我們預約好新聞發佈會的場地了嗎？
Burke: Yes, I have.	有的，我有。
Christina: Have you confirmed all the guests for the press conference tomorrow?	你有確定了所有明天記者發表會的客人了嗎？
Burke: Yes for that too. In case you will ask, all the equipment and food are in order as well.	這個也有。以防妳會問，所有設備還有食物也準備好了。
Christina: Sorry, I am just being nervous, not that I do not trust you.	抱歉，我只是緊張了，不是我不信任你。
Burke: It is alright, but what bothers me is that you asked me to change the subject	沒關係，但是困擾我的是妳要求我要改這場記者會

of this press conference? | 的題目嗎?

Christina: Yes, instead of saying we will be making environmentally-friendly products this year, please announce our cooperation with the "change for good" fundraising program. | 是的,請宣布我們「零錢布施」募款的計畫,以代替原先的今年要開始的環保產品生產計畫。

Burke: But our topic was "Go green", and it was announced. | 但是我們的主題本來是「走向綠色」,而且已經公告了。

I will find a way to twist it back. That is why you need me here for. | 我會找個方法扭轉回來的。這就是為什麼妳需要我在這。

Christina: Thank you, Burke. I will email you the details of the new program in a minute. | 謝謝你 Burke。我等下會把這新的計畫的細節 email 給你。

辦公室篇

貿易篇

業務篇

行銷篇

感情篇

Part 4

辦公室心情隨筆

Christina:

Okay, we need someone like Burke for our company's public relations part. Firstly, I will tell him what we expect from him although he knows I still have to say what I have to say. Okay, he understands what we need him for, and he is confident in himself. He is the good choice for our company. Now I am hoping him to explain the difference between public relations and advertising agencies because what they do just looks similar to me sometimes. After he explained that way, now I get that they are completely different in the way they do things. Okay, now I will ask him to hold next week's press conference, but before that, he needs to sign a non-disclosure agreement with us, since it is the rules.

好，我們需要像 Burke 一樣的人來負責我們公司公關的部分。首先我要告訴他我們期望他什麼，雖然他知道，但是我還是要說我該說的。好，他明白我們需要他什麼，而且他對自己有自信。他對我們公司而言是好的選擇。現在我希望他可以跟我解釋公關和廣告公司的不同處，因為有時候他們做的事情看起來好像。他那樣解釋完後，現在我明白了他們做事的方法是全然不同的。好，現在我要請他主持下禮拜的記者會，但是在那之前，他需要簽一個保密協議，因為那是規定。

Okay, tomorrow is the day for his first press conference for our company. I hope he is doing well. I should not ask, but I just wanted to make sure he got everything under his control. Oh right, we are changing the subject of the press conference tomorrow. I know it is too short-noticed, but I hope he can manage it. Yes, he should be able to keep things going smoothly.

好，明天就是他在我們公司的第一場記者會了，我希望他做得好，我不應該問但我只是想確定一切都在他掌控下。噢對，我們要改明天記者會的題目，我知道這太臨時通知了但是我希望他能處理。對，他應該要能讓事情順利進行。

Burke:

Cristina wants me to work for their company, let me hear her out first. All she is saying are what we were supposed to do, and I happen to be very good at it. Now, I will start to sell myself. Okay, now they really want me for their company. Oh, that question again? Why are so many people confused with these two? Okay, then I will explain to her as I do not want her to work with me but not knowing exactly what I do.

Cristina 想要我替她們公司工作，讓我先聽她怎麼說。她所說的都是些我們本來就該做的事情，而我剛好非常在行。現在我要開始推銷自己了。好，現在他們真的想要我替他們公司工作了。噢，又是那個問題嗎？為什麼有這麼多人會把這兩個搞混？好吧，那我就跟她解釋，因為我不想要她跟我共事卻不知道我到底在做什麼的。

Okay, now she gets it. Finally, it is the signing contract part. A press conference is a piece of cake to me. I can plan it with my eyes close and still run it successfully.

好，現在她懂了。終於到了簽合約這部分了。一個記者會對我來說是小事一樁，我可以閉著眼睛計劃都還能成功進行。

Okay, now she calls a meeting, probably because of the press conference tomorrow, and I must ask her if she is really changing the subject all of the sudden. Now she is asking me some very annoying questions, of course I have all that organized. Okay, now I am asking about the subject of tomorrow's subject. Looks like it is really changing, fine. I will *still try to make it under our earlier announced topic.*

　　好，現在她召開會議，也許是因為明天的記者招待會吧，而且我必須問她是不是真的突然要換題目。現在她在問我一些很煩的問題，我當然安排好那些了。好，現在我要問關於明天的題目了。看來她真的要換，沒關係，我還是會試著把它變成我們稍早前公布的主題底下。

好好用句型

★ **Although I do speaking for living, I will not talk more than I perform.**

雖然我靠說話為生，但我不會光說不做的。

talks more than performs 說的比做的多，即有光說不做之意

　　Or you can say

- all bark and no bite

  只會叫而不會咬。（光說不做之意）

- a man of words and not of deeds

  一個只會說卻沒有行動的人。（意指為光說不做的人）

★ **You have no idea.**

那你大錯特錯了！（在對話中常會聽到，意指對方錯了，且對方還不知道錯在哪裡的感覺）

　　Or you can say:

- Think again!

  再想一次！（說者有認為對方說的或做的是錯的意思，以委婉的方式提醒對方的錯誤）

- You are grossly mistaken.

  你大錯特錯了。

★ **In short, they do "paid media" and we do "free media"**

and "earned media".

簡單來說，他們做的是「付費的媒體」，而我們做的是「免費的媒體」以及「賺來的媒體」。

in short

簡單來説

Or you can say:

- the simple fact is that

  簡單來説

- briefly

  簡言之

 **心理小測試**

交際手腕

Q 在平時的小聚會上，你通常偏好以下哪種飲品呢？

A：紅酒／白酒

B：烈酒

C：雞尾酒／調酒

D：啤酒

測驗結果
請見下頁

測 驗 結 果

A：你是個機會主義者。你對於自己或者朋友都有蠻高的要求，你為人非常進取，一旦遇到對自己有利的人，就會全力出擊，務必讓自己能認識對方，以提升自己的事業和地位，不過妳不是損人利己的人。

B：你是個雙面人。你表面上毫無殺傷力，但實際上卻是個雙面人。剛認識你的人，會被你的外表誤導了，以為你是沒有心機的，但是一旦深入了解你後，會慢慢發現你對於沒有利用價值的人，是會慢慢揭開真面目的。

C：你是個交際高手。你的交際手腕一流，你知道身邊每個人隨時都有可能會是你的貴人，所以你面面俱到，你會迎合不同的人，以備不時之需。

D：你是個性情中人。你把喜歡或不喜歡全寫在臉上，是個完全沒有心機的人，你不會刻意去結交朋友，只要和你談得來就可以是你的朋友。

心理知識補一補

當計畫趕不上變化

曾聽過有人說「計畫永遠趕不上變化，變化抵不上客戶的一通電話。」聽起來讓人有點啼笑皆非，因為這句話正是現今職場上的最佳寫照。無論是科技新貴、公務員還是賣鹽酥雞的老闆都會遇到。我個人就常看到當賣鹽酥雞的老闆問客人要不要辣？客人豪氣的說「要，辣一點。」，正當老闆要灑下去的時候，他又改口說「不要好了。」這時候如果你是老闆，那你是會笑笑地說好，還是送他一個大白眼呢？

這裡要談的不是關於服務精神，而是一個在社會心理學中常會使用到的名詞：「曖昧忍受度」（Tolerance for Ambiguity），這裡指的不是男女感情之間的曖昧，而是指在日常環境當中，個體對於不太明確或是模稜兩可的外在刺激或是事件，例如是上一段提到的鹽酥雞老闆面對的就是：「到底要不要加辣」的問題時的態度，是能以積極的正面態度處理還是將其視為威脅。將這樣混亂狀況以正面思考方式，不當成是威脅的人被認為是曖昧忍受度高。而通常曖昧忍受度高的人，學習能力較強，較容易適應環境。就像對話中的 Burke 一樣，面對客戶臨時抽換主題，仍能面不改色地從容應對。

Unit 5 型男阿Joe 海外派遣

 前情提要

Alex is telling Joe that there is an urgent overseas assignment order in their GY Company in France for him due to staff shortage problems.

Alex 正在告訴 Joe，由於人員短缺的問題，有個讓他去在法國的 GY 公司的緊急調職命令。

 角色介紹

Joe- The marketing manager of GY Company, Taiwan（GY 公司台灣的行銷經理）

Alex- The executive director of GY Company, Taiwan（GY 公司台灣的執行董事）

💬 **情境對話**

Alex: Joe, **do you remember I told you about the staff shortage problem we have?** / Joe 你記得我告訴過你關於人手短缺的問題嗎？

Joe: Yes, you were saying that you might need to send me work in the U.S branch. / 記得啊，你說你們有可能把我送到美國分公司去。

Alex: Yes, about that. Now we are still / 對，關於那個。現在我們

reassigning you oversea, but not U.S, It's France that we want you there.

還是要將你調職到海外，只是不是美國。我們想要你去的是法國。

Joe: What? But I do not speak French, and I studied in the U.S., I will have no problem living in the U.S. Besides, I was not prepared for going to France.

什麼？但是我不會講法文啊，而且我以前在美國唸書的，我去美國生活的話沒問題的。再說，我對於調到法國去並沒有準備好。

Alex: I am sorry, Joe, but this is a done deal.

Joe，我很抱歉，但是這已經是不能改變的事了。

Joe: Well, I don't know what to say.

嗯，我不知道該說什麼了。

Alex: This is a great opportunity for you, as it can widen your sight.

這對你來說是個大好的機會，因為這能擴大你的視野。

Joe: I know all that. It is just too sudden. What exactly will I be doing there? What position?

那些我都知道。只是太突然了。我去那邊確切會做些什麼？什麼職位？

Alex: You will still be a Marketing manager and do what you do here, just in a different environment with different people. You will still report to me though. That will not change.

你還會是個行銷經理，做你在這做的事情，只是在不同的環境，跟不同的人。你還是會要向我報告。這點不會改變。

辦公室篇

貿易篇

業務篇

行銷篇

感情篇

Part 4

Joe: It is good that I will still have you. Any advice for me?

知道我還有你真好。有任何給我的建議嗎？

Alex: Learn French!

學法文！

 前情提要

Joe has left Taiwan to the GY Company in France. Alex is calling to check on Joe.

Joe 離開台灣去法國的 GY 公司了。Alex 打電話去關心 Joe。

 角色介紹

Joe- Formerly the marketing manager of GY Company, Taiwan, now the marketing manager of GY Company, France（以前 GY 公司台灣的行銷經理，現在是 GY 公司法國的行銷經理）

Alex- The executive director of GY Company, Taiwan（GY 公司台灣的執行董事）

 情境對話

Alex: Hey Joe, it's Alex. Are you asleep?

嘿 Joe，是 Alex 啦。你睡著了嗎？

Joe: Alex! I am glad that you called. I am still up. You need me for anything?

Alex！我很高興你打電話來。我還醒著。你找我有事嗎？

Alex: No, I am just calling to see how you are doing.

沒有，我只是打來看你過得好嗎。

型男阿 Joe 海外派遣 Unit 5

辦公室篇

貿易篇

業務篇

行銷篇

感情篇

Joe: I am fine. Actually, I am great. It has been only a month; I am already loving this place.

我沒事。事實上，我很好。才過了一個月，我已經愛上這個地方了。

Alex: Wow! You are adaptable! What changed you?

哇！你適應力真強！是什麼改變了你？

Joe: Well, the working hours here are short and people are friendly, and a lot.

這個嘛，這裡的工作時數短，還有人很友善，以及很多。

Also, **just between you and me**, you remember you say I get to "widen my sight"? It really has. Girls here are pretty and they… let us just say they like to wear skimpy outfits. Besides, people here find my French accent cute.

還有，這是我們私下說的哦，你記得你跟我說我可以「擴展視野」嗎？真的有。這裡的女生都好漂亮，而且她們……，就這麼說吧，她們喜歡穿布料少的衣服。此外，這裡的人覺得我講法文的口音很可愛。

Alex: I totally get what you mean.

我完全明白你的意思了。

Joe: Anyway, do not worry about me. I do not want to go back now.

總之，不用擔心我。我現在不想回去了。

Alex: I am so happy to hear that! Keep in touch, I will let you sleep now.

我很高興聽到你這麼說！保持聯絡，我要讓你去睡覺了。

辦公室心情隨筆

 Alex:

Oh no. Now I have to tell Joe that he will be sent to France instead of the U.S. that he has been waiting for.

噢不。現在我要告訴 Joe 他會被送去法國而不是他一直等待的美國。

This is not easy to tell. Okay, I will talk to him now.

好,我會現在跟他講。

Okay, he is totally surprised and probably shocked, too. He looks so sad and disappointed in me. It is like I did not keep my word, but it is not my call to make. Now I just have to comfort him although it is not working.

好,他完全驚訝了可能嚇到了。他看起來好難過而且對我失望。好像我沒守住我的諾言一樣。但是這不是我能決定的。現在我只需要安撫他就算不管用。

Okay, he is happier when he finds out that he will still works for me. Advice from me? Of course, it is learning French! Language seems to be the biggest barrier when he works there.

好,他知道他還是會為我工作後感到開心了點。要我給建議?當然是學法文!如果他在那工作,語言看來是他最大的障礙。

Okay, it is quite late there in France, Joe has been there for a month already. I want to say Hi and see if he is okay there.

好,在法國蠻晚了,Joe 去那邊已經一個月了,我想打聲招呼然後看看他在那好不好。

Wow, he sounds very happy now, looks like he was not beaten at all, and pretty girls around calling him cute, which is a paradise for him now. Now I have nothing to worry about.

哇,他現在聽起來很快樂,看來他完全沒被打敗,身邊還有漂亮女生說他可愛，這對他現在來說是天堂了。現在我沒什麼好擔心的了。

辦公室篇
貿易篇
業務篇
行銷篇
感情篇

 Joe:

Alex is talking about transferring-me-to-the-U.S. thing, I am all prepared.

Alex 在說的是把我調到美國那件事，我都準備好了。

What? They are sending me to France? Just like that? How can they do this to me? I do not know how to speak French at all and I love the U.S. I guess complaining or crying will not change anything, so I had better just shut my mouth then. Of course, I know it is a good chance for me, but just not what I was told. What will I be doing there then? Still my old stuffs, just a different place and people? He said it easily, but this is a lot. Okay, at least I will still have Alex.

什麼？他們要送我到法國？就那樣？他們怎麼可以這樣對我？我完全不知道怎麼講法文，而且我愛美國。我猜抱怨或者哭都不會改變任何事，所以我還是閉上嘴好了。我當然知道這對我來說是好的機會，只是不是我被告知的。我在那邊要做什麼？做一樣的事情只是同地方不同人？他說得簡單，但是沒那麼簡單。好吧，至少我還有 Alex。

Does he have any recommendations for me? Learn French? Of course, I know that!

他有任何建議要給我嗎？學法文？這個我當然知道！

Wow! It's Alex calling! I miss him! He cares about me, so thoughtful! I must let him know and how happy I am to work here. Let me tell him more so he can get it.

哇！Alex 打來了！我想他！他在乎我真貼心！我一定要讓他知道還有感覺到我在這裡工作有多開心。讓我告訴他更多，他就能明白。

Now he knows why I am so happy here. I will ask him not

to worry.

現在他知道我為什在這裡那麼快樂了。我要叫他別擔心了。

 好好用句型

★ **Do you remember I told you about the staff shortage problem we have?**

你記得我告訴過你關於人手短缺的問題嗎？

staff shortage

人手不足

　　Or you can say:

　　• short-handed

　　　人手短缺

　　• understaffed

　　　人力不足

★ **I do not know what to say.**

我不知道該說什麼了。（有「無言以對」的含意）

　　Or you can say:

　　• I am speechless.

　　　我無言以對了。

　　• I have nothing to say.

　　　我無話可說了。（亦作為無言以對）

★ **Just between you and me.**

我們私下說的。（只現在說的只有你和我知道，也可作為是秘密解釋）

　　Or you can say:

- off the record
  不作紀錄的（也有私下說的意思）
- in private
  私下地

 **心理小測試**

重要首映會的抉擇

Q 假如你期待一場電影首映會很久了，你花了不少錢才得到票，進去還能見到自己的偶像。正當你準備好要出發的時候，你的好朋友打來哭訴，這時候你會？

A：毫不猶豫的跑到他家，陪他度過難關

B：一開始不知道該怎麼做，但跟他聊一陣子發現他情緒不穩定後，決定放棄首映會，去他家陪他

C：先在電話裡穩定他的情緒後，告訴他你有重要的事走不開，晚點去陪他

D：直接跟他說你現在走不開，但是也說明你會另外找時間去看他

測驗結果

A：你是個很懂得幫助別人的人，但常常在朋友需要幫助的時候忽略自己

B：你希望充分維護自己的利益，但又不願意傷害朋友，在自己的利益與朋友的利益之間徘徊不定，因而總是患得患失

C：你十分清楚自己要的是什麼，但同時很少為了取別人而感情用事。遇到問題時，你會很適當的衡量利益，以平衡各方面需求

D：在你和外界之間，你會畫出一道清楚的界線。你是個自我的人，除了自己以外沒有什麼能改變你的意志。

型男阿 Joe 海外派遣　Unit 5

辦公室篇

貿易篇

業務篇

行銷篇

感情篇

心理知識補一補

◈ 陌生環境

　　在心理學中認為，人類習慣處在熟悉的環境，其實是一種自我保護的行為表現。成年人在陌生的環境中儘管比在孩童時期時來的淡定，但其實心中還是會有些微的恐懼或排斥，卻能以理性去加以掩飾或是抑制。

　　而在職場中，總是難免會有新人的加入、職務的調動等，所以常會無可避免地需要接觸到陌生的環境。就如對話中的 Joe 一樣，在知道被派駐到法國之後，由於與其原先認為的美國不同，再加上不通法語，因此造成心中的極大落差，而出現排斥，但在知道在法國的工作、業務進度等還是需向 Alex 報告的時候，了解至少不用適應新的上司，所以接受了派駐。而在新的環境中，因為良好的工作環境因此也加速了他對於陌生環境的適應。

　　所以一般建議在新人加入的時候，可以舉辦迎新活動，對新人釋出善意，也讓新人有機會能與要共事的人談話，並藉由簡單的介紹，找出彼此的共通性，以達到快速適應環境的目的。

Part 5
感情篇

Part 5

Unit 1 如何追求心上人

前情提要

Soo sees Eva when he was beside Nagihan, and Soo wants to ask Eva out the minute he sees her.

Soo 在 Nagihan 旁邊的時候看到 Eva，而 Soo 第一眼看到 Eva 的時候就想追她了。

角色介紹

Soo- Staff 1（職員 1）

Eva- Staff 2（職員 2）

Nagihan- Staff 3（職員 3）

情境對話

Soo: Nagihan, look there! That girl standing there is so cute.

Nagihan 看那邊！那個站在那邊的女生好可愛。

Soo: Do you know where she's from? **I want to ask her out.**

你知道她是哪裡人嗎？我想追求她。

Nagihan: Which one? The girl in the white top over there?

哪一個？那個在那邊穿著白上衣的女生嗎？

Soo: Yes, I think I am falling in love with

對，我想我已經愛上她

her already.

了。

Nagihan: No way! I am prettier; she has got really small eyes.

怎麼會！我比較漂亮，她還有著小眼睛。

Soo: No. I only see long hair and snow white alike skin.
I never felt this way. She is so beautiful.

沒有啊。我只看到長頭髮還有白雪公主一般的肌膚。
我從來沒有這樣的感覺。她好漂亮。

Nagihan: **They are right about beauty is in the eye of the beholder.**

人們說的情人眼裡出西施是對的。

Soo: Nagihan, can you ask her number for me please?

Nagihan 可以拜託妳幫我跟她要號碼嗎？

Nagihan: Do not get me into this. You are on your own.

別把我捲入這個。你靠自己吧。

Soo: Hi, my name is Soo, what is your name?

你好，我的名字是 Soo。妳叫什麼名字？

Eva: I am Eva. What can I help you?

我是 Eva。我能幫你什麼嗎？

Soo: Eva, can I have your number?

Eva 我可以跟妳要妳的電話號碼嗎？

Eva: Sorry, I am busy. Bye.

抱歉，我很忙。再見。

Part 5

 前情提要

Soo runs into Eva again the next day in the office.

Soo 在隔天再次遇到了 Eva。

 角色介紹

Soo- Staff 1（職員 1）

Eva - Staff 2（職員 2）

 情境對話

Soo: Eva, it is me again. Please let me finish. I know this might sound weird, but I have never felt the same about any other girl. I just hope I can be friends with you and get to know you if it is even possible.

Eva，又是我。請讓我說完。我知道這可能聽起來很怪，但是我對其他女生從來沒有這樣的感覺。我希望我可以跟妳成為朋友，甚至可能的話我希望可以了解妳。

Eva: **I know you better than yourself**. You think I am easy.

我把你看透了。你覺得我很容易到手。

Soo: No, you are not. Please just give me your number. Let me take you out for dinner or something. Even a drink is fine. Just give me one chance, please.

不，妳不是。請給我妳的電話，讓我帶妳出去吃晚餐或什麼的。即使是喝個東西也可以。就給我一個機會拜託。

Eva: No. I am sorry I just do not see why I have to.

不，我很抱歉，我不知道我為什麼要。

Will you give me a reason why I must go out with you?
You do not even know me that well.

你能給我一個我必須跟你出去的理由嗎？
你根本也不那麼了解我。

Soo: I will not find out until you give me a chance to.
What can make you go on a date with me?

妳不給我機會的話我就不會知道。
怎麼樣可以讓妳跟我出去約會？

Eva: Not if you have tickets to Maroon 5's concert next week.

除非你有下禮拜魔力紅演場會的票。

Soo: Then you just said yes. I can get us two tickets in. I have my way.

那妳剛剛答應了。我有辦法為我們兩個拿到票。我有我的辦法。

Eva: Good! It is a date then.

很好！那就是個約會囉。

Part 5

辦公室心情隨筆

Soo:

Oh my goodness! That girl over there is just so cute! She is so my type! I think I am in love with her already. She works in the same company as me? How lucky I am! I want to ask her out. Let me share this with Nagihan first. I bet she would also think she is cute.

我的天啊！那個在那邊的女生超可愛的！她完全是我的菜！我覺得我已經愛上她了。她跟我在同公司上班嗎？我真幸運！我想要約她出去。讓我先跟 Nagihan 說。我賭她也會跟我一樣覺得她可愛。

What? Nagihan thinks she is better than that girl? She thinks she is prettier than that girl? In her dream? Is she blind? Oh! I really like her. I wonder if Nagihan is willing to ask that girl's number for me. I am too shy to go there. I can hear my heartbeats.

什麼？Nagihan 覺得她比那女生好？她覺得她比那女生漂亮？在她夢裡嗎？她瞎了嗎？噢！我真的很喜歡她。不知道 Nagihan 會不會願意幫我跟她要號碼。我不好意思過去。我都可以聽到我心跳聲了。

Nagihan does not want to help me. Okay, I will go. Alright she just rejected me. At least now I know her name.

Nagihan 不想幫我。好吧，我去。好吧，她拒絕我了。至少我現在知道她名字了。

Oh! Is Eva! This time I will not leave until I get her number.

噢！是 Eva！這次我不要到號碼我不離開。

She thinks I am some kind of playboy, I guess. I cannot let her misunderstand me. I have to let her know I just want to take her out for dinner if she allows me. She still says no. What? Maroon 5 tickets? Easy for me! Now she finally says yes!

她以為我是什麼花花公子吧，我猜。我不可以讓她誤會我，我必須讓她知道如果她允許的話，我只是想約她出去吃晚餐。她還是說不。什麼？魔力紅的票？對我來說很簡單！現在她終於答應了！

Eva:

I can feel that someone is staring at me right now. Who is that? Does he have a problem or something? I can tell they are talking about me, are they judging me or what? He is making me feel uncomfortable now. He is coming this way, what does he want exactly? He wants my number? What? This is a workplace, what is he thinking? He thinks I am easy to get? I am not that kind of girl. Of course, I will not give him my number. I am not that stupid. I will just tell him I am busy, and I will leave now.

我可以感覺到有人正在盯著我看。那是誰啊？他是有什麼問題還是怎麼樣嗎？我可以看出來他們正在討論我，他們是在評論我嗎還是怎麼樣？他現在讓我感到不舒服。他往這邊走來了。他到底想怎麼樣？他想要我的號嗎？什麼啊？這裡是工作場所，他在想什麼？他以為我很好到手嗎？我才不是那種女生。我當然不會給她我的號碼，我沒那麼笨。我要讓他知道我很忙然後現在離開。

What? Is that guy again! What a bad day! He is coming to me again. I wish I could run now. What else does he want to say? He thinks he can fool me by saying that? I will let him know how I feel about him. Now he looks sincere, but no I still do not want to go out with him. Okay unless you have tickets of the Maroon 5 concert.

什麼？又是那個男的？真是不好的一天！他又向我走來了。我希望我現在可以跑走。他還想些什麼啊？他以為他那樣說可以騙到我嗎？我

辦公室篇

貿易篇

業務篇

行銷篇

感情篇

Part 5

要讓他知道我對他的感覺。現在他看起來蠻真誠的。但我還是不想要跟他出去。好啊，除非你有魔力紅演唱會的票。

What? He has? Looks like he is not that bad then, at least we have the same taste in music.

什麼？他有辦法？看來他也沒那麼糟，至少我們對音樂有相同的品味。

好好用句型

★ **I want to ask her out.**
我想追求她。
ask her out 追求她

> Or you can say:
> - pursue her
>   追求她
> - go after her
>   追求她

★ **They are right about beauty is in the eye of the beholder.**
人們說的情人眼裡出西施是對的。
Beauty is in the eye of the beholder.
情人眼裡出西施。

> Or you can say:
> - Nobody's sweetheart is ugly.
>   情人眼裡出西施。
> - Every lover sees a thousand graces in the beloved object.
>   情人眼裡出西施。

★ **I know you better than yourself.**

我把你看透了

Or you can say:

- I already see you through.

  我已經把你看透了。

- I can read your mind.

  我能讀你的心。（意指能得知對方心理在想些什麼）

心理小測試

邂逅愛情的地方

Q 假如有一天你要對城市旅遊節的來賓送禮物。你會選擇贈送以下哪個？

A：糖果禮盒

B：書籍

C：有紀念意義的 CD

D：旅遊節設計的紀念徽章

測驗結果
請見下頁

辦公室篇

貿易篇

業務篇

行銷篇

感情篇

測 驗 結 果

A：你是個小甜心，對於愛情的幻想停留在城堡中，有旋轉木馬的遊樂場，是你和他／她邂逅的最佳地點。

B：擁有著學院氣息的你。你心裡一定很渴望可以在圖書館裡隔著書架看到那個他／她吧！

C：你喜歡自由，不喜歡拘束，但又很注重生活品質。有品味的藝廊或者街角的咖啡館將會是你和他／她擦出愛情火花的地方。

D：你是個非常循規蹈矩的人。你的他／她會出現在你身邊。想想身邊的人吧！

心理知識補一補

搭訕

　　"How to hook up with a girl?"（要如何與一個女孩搭訕呢？）在心理學當中會提到的無非就是我們已經在前面談到的，例如創造好的第一印象、或是利用情感協調的理論來找出共通點等之類的。也難怪會有人將工作的階段比喻成為婚姻─面試＝曖昧；試用＝交往；正職＝成家。

　　有一位心理學家將搭訕的方式分做三大類：
- 單刀直入：以最直接的方式，告訴對方，你想要認識她，想要跟她要電話，或是更直接地約她出去。
- 顧左右而言他：以聊天氣、問候、或是提出一些與她個人訊息無關的問題，以掩飾想要跟她搭訕的目的。
- 裝瘋賣傻：以自以為幽默的方式，引起對方的注意，再用話術約她出去，這一點必較像是我們說的「虧美眉」。

　　在對話當中，Eva 對於 Soo 的主動搭訕本來有點反感，但最終卻因為魔力紅的演唱會票而被打動。我猜 Eva 的反感可能是來自於 Soo 偷看她時的眼光，可能太過猥褻了，或是 Soo 有流口水！而最後只能說是情感協調理論勝了，他們找到了共通點，畢竟感情這檔事，是外人說不清的啊！

辦公室篇

貿易篇

業務篇

行銷篇

感情篇

Part 5

Unit 2 女追男隔層紗

前情提要

Olivia shares the same office with Peter, and she has been watching Peter for a while now. She thinks Peter is the good boyfriend material. She has decided to take some moves today.

Olivia 和 Peter 共用一間辦公室。而她觀察 Peter 有一陣子了。她覺得 Peter 是個很適合當男朋友的人。她今天決定採取一些動作。

角色介紹

Olivia: Staff 1（職員 1）
Peter: Staff 2（職員 2）

情境對話

Olivia: Hi Peter, I am Olivia. I am sitting right behind you. We have never talked but I would like us to be friends if you do not mind.

嗨 Peter。我是 Olivia。我就坐在你正後方。我們從沒講過話，但是如果你不介意的話我希望我們能當朋友。

Peter: Hi Olivia, okay sure.

嗨 Olivia。好啊，沒問題。

Olivia: **I think my computer is out of**

我想我的電腦壞掉了，可

254

女追男隔層紗 Unit 2

辦公室篇

貿易篇

業務篇

行銷篇

感情篇

order, can you have a look at it for me please? | 以拜託你幫我看一下嗎？

Peter: Not a problem. There you go. It is functioning now. | 不成問題。給妳。現在可以運作了。

Olivia: Wow, you are really good with computers! If it is okay with you, I have a laptop in my place also needs to be fixed… | 哇，你對電腦真的很在行。如果可以的話，我家還有一台筆電要修……

Peter: You want me to your place? | 妳想要我去妳家嗎？

Olivia: No, I am thinking whether or not I can bring that to the office to you tomorrow. | 不是，我是想說我明天可不可以帶來辦公室給你。

Peter: Actually, I was thinking to go to your place to fix it, so you do not have to take the heavy laptop to the office. | 事實上，我在想我可以去妳家修理，那麼妳就不用搬這麼重的筆電來辦公室。

Olivia: **You have a way with woman!** But no, thanks, my parents will always be home, so it is not a good idea. | 你對女人真有一套！但是不了，謝謝，我父母總是在家，這不是個好主意。

Peter: Alright, I will see you and your laptop tomorrow then. | 好，那麼跟妳和妳的筆電明天見囉。

Olivia: Than you, Peter. | 謝謝你，Peter。

Part 5

 前情提要

The next day Olivia brings her laptop to the office to Peter and today happens to be Peter's birthday. Olivia has something hidden in her laptop for Peter.

隔天 Olivia 帶她的電腦到辦公室給 Peter，今天剛好也是 Peter 的生日。Olivia 藏了些東西在她電腦裡要給 Peter。

 角色介紹

Olivia: Staff 1（職員 1）
Peter: Staff 2（職員 2）

 情境對話

Olivia: Hi, Peter, here is the laptop that I mentioned. You will have to turn the laptop on to see if it is working.

嗨，Peter。這是我提到的筆電。你會需要開電腦看是不是可以用。

Peter: Hi, Olivia. You really brought your laptop here. Yes, I will have to boost up your laptop to check first. Do you have secrets inside that you are afraid to let me see?

嗨，Olivia。妳真的帶妳的電腦來這裡了。是的，我要先開機看妳檢查妳的電腦。妳裡面有秘密害怕被我看到的嗎？

Olivia: I am not sure. Probably! However, I do know, if you turned it on later, it will shows a report that I recently typed.

我不確定。可能哦！然而我確定的是，如果你等下打開了，它會顯示一個我最近打的報告。

Peter: That sounds boring though. I was expecting something interesting.
Okay, now let us see... The laptop seems alright. And here is the report you were saying... it starts with "Dear Peter"... me?

那聽起來蠻無聊的。我本來是期待更有趣的。
好。現在讓我們來看……筆電看起來沒是啊……然後這裡這個就是妳說的那個報告……開頭是「親愛的 Peter」……我？

Olivia: **I think you just found yourself a sugar report.**

我想你剛剛幫你自己找到了情書。

Peter: Is this for me? And it also says Happy Birthday, how do you know that?

這是給我的嗎？而且還寫著生日快樂，妳怎麼知道？

Olivia: Yes, it is for you. And we have a booklet that shows everyone's birthday. It is not hard to find out.
I really like you Peter. I know it might sounds creepy, but I have been watching you. Are you interested in spending your birthday with me tonight?

是，是給你的。然後我們有小冊子上面有每個人的生日，不難發現。
Peter 我真的喜歡你。我知道聽起來可能蠻恐怖的，但是我一直有在注意你。你有興趣今晚跟我一起過你的生日嗎？

Peter: Yes, I am. I am touched.

有。我很感動。

Part 5

 辦公室心情隨筆

 Olivia:

I really like Peter, and I am sick of just sitting here and watch him. Okay, I will start by talking to him first. Since my computer is broken now. Let me see if he can fix my computer for me. Before that I want to ask him to be my friend.

我真的喜歡 Peter。我受夠了就只是坐在這看著他。好，我會從跟他說話開始。既然我的電腦現在壞掉了。讓我看看我可不可以讓他幫我修我的電腦。在那之前我想要叫他當我朋友。

Cool, he just fixed it easily. Now I like him more. I do not want this conversation just end like this. Perhaps he is okay to have a look at my laptop from home too? Though it is not broken I can still use it as an excuse.

酷，他輕鬆修好了。現在我更喜歡他了。我不想這個對話就這樣結束。也許他可以看看我家的筆電？雖然沒壞掉但是還是可以用它當藉口。

Okay, he said yes again. Tomorrow I will bring my laptop to the office then, and tomorrow is his birthday I want to use tomorrow as a chance to tell him my feeling for him.

好，他又說好了。那麼明天我要帶我的筆電去辦公室，然後明天是他生日，我希望趁明天當作一個機會告訴他我對他的感受。

Now I will give him my laptop, hopes he can find out about the letter I typed for him.

現在我要給他我的電腦了，希望他趕快發現我打給他的信。

He was not unhappy, then I asked if he would like to have his birthday with me then. Now he said another yes!

他沒有不開心。然後我問了他願不願意跟我一起過他的生日。現在他又答應了！

Peter:

This girl is quite cute, how come I have never paid attention to her? She wants us to be friends, why not? Her computer is broken? I am the expert of computers. It is easy.

這女的蠻可愛的，為什麼我都從沒注意到她？她想要我們當朋友，為何不呢？她的電腦壞掉了？我是電腦專家，這很簡單。

Alright, I got her wrong. However I am okay to go fix her laptop at her place because a laptop is heavy. Okay then, if her parents will be home, that will be quite awkward.

噢，我誤會她了。然而我還是可以去她家修筆電，因為一台筆電很重。好吧，如果她父母會在家，那會還蠻尷尬的。

What? What report? So boring! Okay, now I will turn the laptop on now. Why is it not broken at all? There is the report she said. Why do I see my name on it? Is it for me? No way! It also says happy birthday and today is my birthday. What? Is it really me? I am so touched. How would she like me? She is asking me for spending my birthday with her. Okay, I will give us a shot then.

什麼？什麼報告？真無聊！好，現在我來開筆電。為什麼根本沒壞？這是她說的那個報告。為什麼我看到上面有我的名字？是要給我的嗎？不可能！上面還寫生日快樂而今天是我生日。什麼？這真的是我？我好感動。她怎麼會喜歡我呢？她要我跟她一起過我的生日，好。我就給我們一個機會。

好好用句型

★ **I think my computer is out of order.**

我想我的電腦壞掉了

out of order

壞掉了（形容電器產品類）

> Or you can say:

- out of whack

  不正常（形容電器產品類）

- busted

  壞掉了（例如：busted cellphone screen 破掉的手機螢幕；但用在形容人的話，則當作被當場逮到，或是被破梗之意。）

★ **You have a way with women.**

你對女人真有一套

> Or you can say:

- You have a gift with the ladies.

  你對女人真有一套

- He is good with the ladies.

  你對女人真有一套

★ **I think you just found yourself a sugar report.**

我想你剛剛幫你自己找到了情書。

sugar report

情書

> Or you can say:

- love letter

  情書

- love notes
  情書

 心理小測試

戀人的個性

Q 總公司下派了一位新主管到你所在的公司，在他正式上任之前，同事們就傳聞他有一個故事，雖然你不喜歡八卦，但是你也不自覺的瞎猜，你認為傳聞會是什麼？

A：年輕的時候，他很想改變貧困山區的教育狀況，因此曾經有志願當過教師的經驗。

B：年輕時剛進公司就指責過上司錯誤，但現在他自己又犯了相同的錯誤。

C：單身時，將自己的功勞讓給了家裡有困難的同事，而失去了晉升的機會。

D：他年輕時候是個吃軟飯的人，如果沒有老婆的幫忙，就什麼都不是。

測 驗 結 果

A：你喜歡那種無論是在精神上或肉體上都配合你的人，你正在尋找一個可以依靠的人。

B：你喜歡那種有冷靜的頭腦，在工作上能力很強的人，因此你的緣份大多會在工作環境中產生。

C：你喜歡溫柔體貼的人。

D：你喜歡富有母（父）性的人，喜歡對你有依賴，長的可愛的人。

心理知識補一補

◆◆ 女追男真的隔層紗嗎？

　　誰說女追男真的隔層紗？如果拿古代流傳下的故事來看，好像並沒有這麼地容易。例如白蛇傳中的許仙及白娘子，在鎮江的說書版本中，白娘子可是等了許仙又一次的輪迴後，又是安排巧遇，又是給他銀兩後才成親的。而梁山伯與祝英台的故事中，祝英台的追夫之路算得上是坎坷吧，最後還要跑到男方家告訴梁山伯她是女的才成功，後面的蝴蝶就不談了。還有一個晉朝時出於搜神後記的故事「田螺姑娘與謝端」，說的是謝端撿了一個田螺後，便將其養在水缸中，而這一個田螺姑娘每天為他煮飯、打掃，最後被他發現了才成親。這田螺姑娘也太辛苦了吧！還沒結婚就先操持家務了，讓人不禁懷疑女追男真的容易嗎？

　　如果就心理學的層面來看，男人有勇氣或是願意直接拒絕主動追求的女性為少數，而男人也較不掩飾自己的生理慾望，所以才會有隔層紗的說法。但就這一個男女平權的時代而言，應該已經對於「誰追誰」沒有什麼限制了。我只能說沒有付出，哪有收穫！像是 Olivia 不就是費了一番心思，才讓 Peter 注意到她。所以女孩們，喜歡就去追吧！

辦公室篇

貿易篇

業務篇

行銷篇

感情篇

Unit 3 和主管拍拖行不行

 前情提要

Stephen is waiting for Anya to get off work, so he can take her out for dinner.

Stephen 在等 Anya 下班，他就可以帶她出去吃晚餐。

 角色介紹

Anya- Stephen's secretary（Stephen 的秘書）
Stephen- Anya's manager（Anya 的主管）

 情境對話

Stephen: Anya, are you finishing off now?　Anya 妳結束了嗎？

Anya: Not yet, I still need some time I think.　還沒，我想我還需要些時間。

Stephen: Okay, I can wait.　好吧，我可以等。

Anya: Me? Why would you do that? Do not pressure me.　我？你為什麼要那樣做？別給我壓力。

Stephen: Nothing, just I heard there is a new Italian restaurant.　沒什麼。只是我聽說那邊有新開一家義大利餐廳。

Anya: Is it nice? Where about? Italian food is my favorite.

不錯嗎？大概在哪裡啊？義大利菜是我的最愛。

Stephen: I know. Therefore, if you don't have any dinner plan tonight, would you like to have dinner with me at that new Italian restaurant?

我知道。因此如果妳今晚沒有任何晚餐計劃。妳要跟我一起去那家新開的義大利餐廳用餐嗎？

Anya: And it is your treat right?

而且會是你請客對嗎？

Stephen: Yes, it is my treat, since last time you paid for me. **That makes us even now.**

對。我請客。因為上次我讓妳幫我付錢。這樣我們現在就扯平了。

Anya: Alright, I will go with you as soon as I am done with my work of the day.
Okay, we can go now. I am starving.

好。那等我把今天的工作做完就跟你一起去。
好了，我們可以走了。我餓慘了。

Stephen: Let us go now.

現在我們走吧。

Anya: Wow. You forgot to mention the price here is very high?

哇。你忘了提到說這裡的價錢非常高嗎？

Stephen: With girls nowadays, it is no money, no honey.

現在的女孩子，沒錢就沒愛情。

Anya: Not for me!

對我而言不是！

辦公室篇

貿易篇

業務篇

行銷篇

感情篇

Part 5

 前情提要

Stephen and Anya just finished their dinner. They are now discussing where to go next.

Stephen 和 Anya 剛吃完他們的晚餐。他們現在在討論接下來要去哪裡。

 角色介紹

Anya- Stephen's secretary（Stephen 的秘書）

Stephen- Anya's manager（Anya 的主管）

 情境對話

Stephen: How was your dinner?	妳的晚餐如何？
Anya: It was lovely, thank you.	很可口，謝謝你。
Stephen: Do you want to go for a ride now?	妳想去兜個風嗎？
Anya: I would like to go home now.	我現在想回家了。
Stephen: How about we go to my place, and I will make you some tea.	不如我們去我家？我泡茶給妳喝。
Anya: No, it is getting late now.	不要。已經很晚了。
Stephen: How about we go for a walk then?	還是我們去散散步嗎？
Your eyes are as beautiful as the moon tonight.	妳的眼睛像今晚的月亮一樣美。
I will give you a ride home right after	妳跟我散步後我馬上送妳

you walk with me.	回家。
Anya: Okay then.	好吧。
Stephen: Look! There is a hot spring! Do you want to go to that hot spring with me?	看！那裡有溫泉！妳想要跟我一起去泡溫泉嗎？
Anya: **Do not play the same old game,** Stephen. I know what you are up to. Nothing will happen between us, and nothing is going to happen between us tonight. I would like to keep things professional between us.	別老套了 Stephen。我知道你想做什麼。 我們之間不會有什麼，而今晚我們之間也不會發生什麼事。 我希望我們之間保持專業的關係。
Stephen: No one will find out as long as we keep a low profile.	只要我們保持低調就不會有人發現的。
Anya: I am not taking any risks losing my job. Now, take me home.	我不要承擔任何會讓我失去工作的風險。現在，帶我回家。
Stephen: Okay.	好。

辦公室篇

貿易篇

業務篇

行銷篇

感情篇

Part 5

 辦公室心情隨筆

 Stephen:

There is a new Italian restaurant opening not far from here. I know Anya loves Italian food. I will go and see if she is getting off work soon.

那裡有家新的義大利餐廳開幕，離這不遠。我知道 Anya 愛義大利菜，我去看她是不是快下班了。

Okay, she just needs some more time. I can wait. She does not want me to wait, but let me just tell her about the new Italian restaurant.

好，她需要更多時間，我可以等。她不想要我等，但是讓我告訴她關於新義大利餐廳的事。

Now she is interested in going out for dinner with me.

現在她有興趣要跟我出去吃晚餐了。

Now we are here. I did not forget to mention the price as I know if Anya knew the price is that high, she would probably not come with me. I thought all girls are the same that they love rich man. Okay, she seems to be not one of them.

我們到了。我並不是忘記提價錢，只是因為我知道如果 Anya 知道這裡這麼貴，她也許就不會要跟我來了。我以為所有女孩都一樣喜歡有錢男人。她看起來好像並不是這種人。

Now we finished dinner, and I do not want the night to end like this. I will see if she wants to go for a ride. Okay, now she is making it very clear that she does not want to cross the line. Okay, then, I will get her home now.

現在吃完晚餐了，我不想以這種方式結束今晚。我要看她要不要跟我去兜風。好，現在她把話講很清楚，她不想越線。好吧，我現在送她回家。

辦公室篇

貿易篇

業務篇

行銷篇

感情篇

Anya:

Why is Stephen waiting for me? He is not helping me for getting my work done soon. Wow, a new Italian restaurant, now that attracts me! If it is a free treat, then why not? I still have to have dinner anyway.

為什麼 Stephen 要等我？他也沒有在幫我讓我能趕快完成工作。哇，一家新的義大利餐廳，現在就吸引我了！如果是免費招待，那幹嘛不要？我還是要吃晚餐的。

Okay, we can go now. I am so hungry I can eat a cow. What? This restaurant is so expensive. Why did he just say that? He thinks just because he is rich he can get whatever girl he wants? How arrogant!

好，我們現在可以走了。我好餓我可以吃下一整頭牛。什麼？這家餐廳好貴。他剛剛為什麼那樣說？他認為因為他有錢就可以得到任何他想要的女孩嗎？真是自大！

The dinner was good but can I go home now? He really thinks he can get every girl. He just asked me to go to his place, just like that. I am so glad I did not start anything with him yet. Now he wants to go for a walk? What moon? Where did he copy that stupid line? Now he is asking me to go to hot springs with him? It is enough, I cannot stand this anymore, I have to make things straight with him. I want him to understand that in the future it will only be businesses between us. Finally, he is taking me to my place,

晚餐很好，但是我可以回家了嗎？他真的以為他可以得到每個女孩。他剛問我要不要去他家，就那樣問了。我很慶幸我還沒有跟他有任何開始。現在他要散步？什麼月亮？他去哪裡學那麼愚蠢的台詞？現在他要我跟他去泡溫泉？真是夠了，我不能忍受了，我要跟他把話說明

Part 5

白。我要他明白以後我跟他之間只會有公事。終於他要載我回我家了。

🔧 好好用句型

★ **That makes us even now.**

這樣我們現在就扯平了。

We are even.

我們扯平了。

> Or you can say:
> - Fair and fair alike.
>
>   扯平囉。
> - We are even-steven.
>
>   我們互不相欠了。

★ **I will give you a ride home right after you walk with me**

妳跟我散步後我馬上送妳回家

give you a ride 搭便車

> Or you can say:
> - give you a lift
>
>   順道帶你一程
> - offer transportation
>
>   提供交通（有讓人搭便車的意思）

★ **The same old game.**

還是老套

> Or you can say:
> - It's cliché.
>
>   真是陳腔濫調。

- It is old-fashioned.
  真老套。

 心理小測試

暗戀指數

Q 假如有天你和一群人在外地出差，你們相約一起去聚餐，其中有你正在暗戀的人，此時你會點什麼飲料？

A：香濃的印度奶茶

B：甘醇的藍山咖啡

C：色彩繽紛的鮮水果茶

D：清涼簡單的冰綠茶

E：健康原味的鮮榨柳橙汁

F：芳香的熱紅茶

G：滋味獨特的雞尾酒

H：點香甜的霜淇淋來吃

測驗結果
請見下頁

測驗結果

A：被暗戀指數 40%。你無法真正表達內心的情感，有時會表錯情，也容易因為表達不對而錯失良機。

B：被暗戀指數 60%。你面對喜歡的人能侃侃而談，但無法表達出愛意，雖然常常被愛慕，但總是曖昧不明。

C：被暗戀指數 90%。熱情幽默的你，有招蜂引蝶的特性，唯獨在感情上有點弱智，但也是你迷人的一點，你容易被暗戀而有時卻不自知。

D：被暗戀指數 20%。你純真善良，不太打扮，也不懂言語暗示，十分缺乏打動異性的魅力，較容易成為只是談心的朋友。

E：被暗戀指數 70%。隨和風趣的你很有自己的想法，被朋友崇拜和愛慕的機會不少，不過喜歡你的人多數會以暗示的方式表露。

F：被暗戀指數 50%。中規中矩的你很善解人意，雖然不夠浪漫有趣，但能給對方安全感，相處時間一長，就容易被你的個性吸引。

G：被暗戀指數 80%。你擁有獨特神秘感，懂得散發自己的魅力，也擅長大膽的用言語挑逗對方，被愛慕的機會很多，桃花不斷。

H：被暗戀指數 35%。你直爽而俏皮，有點任性但沒心機，對於愛情害羞，有時候會被暗戀，但是大多是你暗戀他人。

 心理知識補一補

刺蝟法則

　　在這裡要注意的是，在這裡談的「刺蝟法則」（Hedgehog Effect）因為名稱相近，常常容易會跟「刺蝟原則」（Hedgehog Principle）搞混。「刺蝟法則」又可稱作是刺蝟效應，在心理學上的定義為人際交往中的心理距離。

　　所謂的「刺蝟法則」是來自於生物學家的一個試驗，他們將一群刺蝟放在寒冷的環境當中，這一群刺蝟會因為寒冷而互相靠近取暖，但又因為身上的刺會刺痛彼此，所以又分開，因為寒冷又會慢慢地靠近，如此反覆幾次之後，會找到一個適當的距離取暖，但又不至於刺傷對方。這一個法則被廣泛地應用在管理實踐上，而在論語顏淵篇中有記載：「齊景公問政於孔子。孔子對曰，君君臣臣，父父子子。」則是與這一個法則所說明的是一樣的，指的是上司及部屬之間因為要一起工作，所以要保持有如朋友之間的關係，但要適當地保持心理距離，以免因為過於親密，而造成工作執行上的困難。

　　在對話當中上司追求女職員，最後是 Anya 以 "I would like to keep things professional between us." 巧妙地拒絕了 Stephen，也因此適當地保持了彼此的心理距離。但是與上司或是部屬談戀愛到底行不行？就只能看個人修行囉！

辦公室篇

貿易篇

業務篇

行銷篇

感情篇

Unit 4 有小三, Line 這麼說

 前情提要

Avery discovered something about Gunnar, and he is telling Scarlett about it in "Line".

Avery 發現了關於 Gunnar 的事情,而她要在"Line"裡面告訴 Scarlett 這個。

 角色介紹

Scarlett- The girlfriend and Zoey's best friend(女朋友以及 Zoey 最好的朋友)

Avery- Scarlett and Gunnar's friend(Scarlett 和 Gunnar 的朋友)

Gunnar- The boyfriend and a manager(男朋友以及經理)

Zoey- Scarlett's best friend and Gunnar's secretary(Scarlett 最好的朋友和 Gunnar 的秘書)

 情境對話

Avery: Scarlett, remember I told you to keep your ears to the ground?　　Scarlett,記得我告訴妳要提高警覺嗎?

Scarlett: About what?　　關於什麼?

Avery: Gunnar and Zoey. I told you I felt　　Gunnar 和 Zoey。我告

something was on between them.

訴過妳我感覺到他們之間有什麼。

Scarlett: Yeah, and I told you there is no way that they will ever betray me.

嗯。然後我跟妳說他們兩個不可能會背叛我。

Avery: God... I do not know how to tell you this... **I want to punch him!**

天啊……我不知道該怎麼告訴妳……我想揍他！

Scarlett: What are you talking about? What happened?

妳在說什麼？發生什麼事了？

Avery: I saw them kissing with my own eyes last night outside of their office.
I do not want to keep anything from you, so I choose to let you know.
Anyway, I think it is not that simple. You will need to ask him to find out.

我親眼看到他們昨天晚上在他們辦公室外面接吻。我不想對妳隱瞞任何事情，所以我選擇讓妳知道。總之，我認為不是那麼簡單的。妳需要問他才會知道。

Scarlett: No, that is not possible. Gunnar is not like that... and Zoey... she is my best friend.

不。那是不可能的。Gunnar 不是那樣的……還有 Zoey……她是我最好的朋友.

Avery: Scarlett, you can keep lying to yourself or you can find out the truth yourself.

Scarlett，妳可以繼續騙自己，或者妳可以自己找出事實。

Part 5

Scarlett: How?

怎麼做？

Avery: Just ask him!

就問他啊！

Scarlett: It is not that simple. If I ask and it turns out to be true, then we will really be over.

這不是那麼簡單的。如果我問了而且如果是真的，那我們就會真的結束了。

Avery: I know this is hard, but go and ask him.

我知道這很難，但是去問他吧。

 前情提要

Scarlett is going to ask Gunnar whether he is having an affair with her best friend Zoey in "Line".

Scarlett 要在"Line"裡面問 Gunnar 他是不是和她最好的朋友 Zoey 有外遇。

 角色介紹

Scarlett- The girlfriend and Zoey's best friend（女朋友以及 Zoey 最好的朋友）

Avery- Scarlett and Gunnar's friend（Scarlett 和 Gunnar 的朋友）

Gunnar- The boyfriend and a manager（男朋友以及經理）

Zoey- Scarlett's best friend and Gunnar's secretary（Scarlett 最好的朋友和 Gunnar 的秘書）

 情境對話

Scarlett: Gunnar, are you there?

Gunnar，你在嗎？

Gunnar: Yes.

嗯。

Scarlett: I do not want to make a scene, so I am asking you something here.

我不想大吵大鬧所以我想在這裡問你一些事情。

Gunnar: What is it? Are you alright?

是什麼？妳沒事吧？

Scarlett: I want you to be honest with me. Avery saw you and Zoey kissing outside the office, is it true?

我要你對我老實說。Avery 看到你和 Zoey 在辦公室外面接吻。這是真的嗎？

Gunnar: Scarlett, I really love you, and there is no one like you.

Scarlett，我真的很愛妳。沒人比得上妳。

Scarlett: Save the sweet talk! Is it true or not?

別在那邊甜言蜜語！這是不是真的？

Gunnar: Yes⋯ it is true. I do not want you to find out this way.

是⋯⋯是真的。我不想要妳以這種方式知道的。

Scarlett: How could you? With all the people in the world, you have to pick her?

你怎麼可以？世上所有的人裡，你一定要選她？

Gunnar: I am so sorry⋯ I do not love her⋯ but there is more to it.

我很抱歉⋯⋯我不愛她⋯⋯但是事情不是那麼簡單。

Part 5

Scarlett: **Do not tell me you that you got her pregnant!**　不要告訴我你讓她懷孕了！

Gunnar: It was just that one time… I am so sorry, Scarlett.　那只是那麼一次……。Scarlett，我很抱歉。

Scarlett: You two are disgusting! I do not even want to know the details.　你們兩個好噁心！我一點也不想知道細節。

 辦公室心情隨筆

 Scarlett:

What is Avery trying to say? He is making me feel so scared and nervous. Why do I have a bad feeling?

Avery 想要說什麼啊？她讓我感覺好害怕好緊張。為什麼我有種不好的感覺？

What? No! Not possible! Of all people in the world I trust them the most! There must be some kind of misunderstandings! But Gunnar has been avoiding me lately. No, this is not possible. This is not true. They cannot be! They can never do this to me. Okay, Avery is right. I got to find out the truth myself. Yes, I will ask him. I will ask him calmly. I am scared of the truth, but I'd also rather not to live in lies.

什麼？不！不可能！他們是全世界我最相信的人！這一定有什麼誤會！但是 Gunnar 最近都在躲我。不，這是不可能的。這不是真的。他們不可能是！他們永遠不可能這樣對我。好吧，Avery 是對的。我需要親自找出真相。對，我會問他。我會冷靜的問他。我害怕真相，但我也寧願不要活在謊言中。

Okay, I am going to ask Gunnar now. Why is he not answering my question? He normally avoids my questions because he does not want to answer it. No, this does not feel good.

好，我現在要去問 Gunnar。為什麼他不回答我的問題？他通常逃避我的問題是因為不想回答。不，這感覺不太對。

Oh my gosh, it is true! How could he? He and my best friend? Why her? Why they did this to me? What is more? I thought kissing is the end of the story. What? This is so disgusting! They are even having a baby? When were they planning on telling me this? No. I want no more details. I am out.

我的天啊，這居然是真的！他怎麼能？他和我最好的朋友？為什麼是她？為什麼這樣對我？還有什麼？我以為接吻就是故事的結尾了。什麼？這真是噁心！他們甚至要有小孩了？他們打算什麼時候要告訴我？不。我不想要更多細節了。我退出。

Gunnar:

Scarlett sounds weird. Is she okay? What is she trying to ask me? Now she wants me to be honest. This is bad. Something must be wrong.

Scarlett 聽起來很怪。她還好嗎？她是想問我什麼？現在她要我誠實。這不太對。一定是出了什麼事了。

Oh, no. Why would Avery saw us? I have to comfort her first. I do not want to lose her. I have to let her know how much I love her and how special she is to me before I say more.

噢，不。為什麼 Avery 會看到我們？我必須先安撫她，我不想失去她。在我說更多之前，我要讓她知道我有多愛她，還有她對我來說有多特別。

Okay, she is all mad now. she is not hearing me say anything but the truth. I just committed a mistake that every man in the world would make.

好，她完全生氣了，她現在不聽我說任何事了，除非是事實。我只是犯了全天下男人都會犯的錯。

Okay I will admit it. It is not like that. I did not choose her and I did not plan of any of this. It just happened. It was an accident. I feel so sorry, but now since she brought this up. I have to tell her more. I have to tell her there is more.

好吧，我承認。不是那樣的。我沒有選擇她，我也沒有計畫任何這些。就是發生了。那只是一個意外。我覺得很抱歉，但是既然她提起了這個。我必須告訴她更多。我不得不告訴她還有更多。

She is right, I got Zoey pregnant. It was the only one time we both got drunk and it just happened. I do not have any feelings for Zoey. I know it's unacceptable to her. Okay, I will say no more. It is over.

她說對了，我讓 Zoey 懷孕了。那是唯一的一次我們都喝醉了然後就發生了。我對 Zoey 沒有任何的感覺。我知道這對她而言是不能接受的。好，我不會再說更多了。結束了。

好好用句型

★ **Remember I told you to keep your ears to the ground**？
記得我告訴妳要提高警覺嗎？

Keep your ears to the ground.
你要提高警覺。

　Or you can say:

- You have to be on your toes.
  你要隨時保持警覺。

- Keep your guard up.
  你要隨時注意。

★ **I want to punch him.**
我想揍他。
punch him 揍他/揍他一頓
  Or you can say:
  - Give him a black eye.
    給他一個「黑輪」。
  - Give him a knuckle sandwich.
    給他迎面一拳。

★ **Do not tell me you that you got her pregnant!**
不要告訴我你讓她懷孕了！
She is pregnant.
她懷孕了。
  Or you can say:
  - She is in the family way.
    她懷孕了。
  - She is in trouble.
    她有麻煩了。（也有「她懷孕了」的說法）

心理小測試

無情指數

Q 當你一個人在看動物頻道時,以下哪一幕的畫面你會最喜歡看?

A:海豚跳躍戲水

B:猴子在樹上嬉戲玩耍

C:老虎獅子在捕捉獵物

D:狐狸一家溫馨依偎著彼此

E:一群小鳥展翅高飛

測驗結果
請見下頁

測驗結果

A：你的無情指數有 **55%**。你是屬於如果確定彼此沒有未來，就會選擇默默離開的人。

B：你的無情指數有 **99%**。你是屬於一旦自己變心了，就會永不回頭的人。

C：你的無情指數有 **40%**。你是屬於只要覺得彼此之間還有任何一絲希望，就不會放棄的人。

D：你的無情指數有 **80%**。你是屬於當對對方忍無可忍時，就會快斬情絲的人。

E：你的無情指數有 **20%**。你會因為還有愛且自己又心軟，而狠不下心斬情絲的人。

辦公室篇

貿易篇

業務篇

行銷篇

感情篇

Unit 5 尷尬總在分手後

前情提要

Vivienne and Kelvin are in an office relationship, and now they are ending this.

Vivienne 和 Kelvin 在談一段辦公室戀情，而他們現在要結束這段戀情。

角色介紹

Vivienne- The girlfriend（女朋友）

Kelvin- The boyfriend（男朋友）

情境對話

Kelvin: I saw you flirting with a client in the office today. 　我看到妳今天跟一個客戶在辦公室調情。

Vivienne: You always see it that way. **Who is to blame for this?** 　你總是那樣看。這件事該怪誰？

Kelvin: I swear to god it is your problem. You are being unprofessional. 　我對上天發誓這是妳的問題。妳現在很不專業。

Vivienne: **There you go again! Will you please stop being childish?** 　你又來了！可以拜託別再小孩子氣了嗎？

I am so sick of explaining myself when 　我厭倦了當根本沒什麼需

there is actually nothing for me to explain.	要解釋的時候，我還要解釋。
Kelvin: Just be cool, alright. I just want you to stop acting like you are single.	冷靜點好嗎。我只是想要妳別再演得好像妳是單身一樣。
Vivienne: That is not the point. The point is I am not. You know what? It is my bad, alright? You and I. it is not going to work.	那不是重點。問題是我沒有。你知道嗎？算我的錯，好嗎？你跟我，是行不通的。
Kelvin: What are you up to?	妳想要幹什麼？
Vivienne: I do not know what you want from me. But I cannot take it anymore.	我不知道你想要我怎麼樣。但是我不能再忍受了。
I am so over with you being paranoid all the time.	我很受夠你總是疑神疑鬼的。
I cannot work like this. Not with you. I have no more patience with you.	我這樣無法工作。不能跟你一起。我對你已經無法容忍了。
Kelvin: That makes the two of us. Whatever got to be, got to be.	彼此彼此。該來的總會來的。
Vivienne: Goodbye, Kelvin. This will not affect our work, right?	再見了 Kelvin。這不會影響我們的工作，對嗎？

Part 5

Kevin: No worries. I am sure we can get through this.

別擔心。我確定我們可以渡過的。

 前情提要

Three months after Vivienne and Kelvin's break up, they are running into each other outside of their company, and Vivienne's new boyfriend is also with her.

Vivienne 和 Kelvin 分手後三個月。他們在 Vivienne 新男朋友在旁邊的時候，在公司外遇到彼此。

 角色介紹

Vivienne- The ex-girlfriend of Kelvin（Kelvin 的前女友）

Kelvin- The ex-boyfriend of Vivienne（Vivienne 的前男友）

Adrian- The new boyfriend of Vivienne（Vivienne 的新男友）

 情境對話

Kelvin: Hi Vivienne, it has been a while. You look good.

嗨，Vivienne，已經有一陣子了吧。妳看起來不錯。

Vivienne: Thank you. This is my new boyfriend, Adrian.

謝謝你。這是我的新男朋友，Adrian。

Kelvin: Thanks for sharing. Well, this is a bit awkward.

謝謝妳告訴我。嗯。這有點尷尬。

Vivienne: Come on, we have moved past that.

拜託。我們已經忘了那個了。

Kelvin: Not me. I am still having a bad time. I am not over you, Vivienne.

我沒有。我還是過的不好。我還沒忘了妳，Vivienne。

Vivienne: You cannot always get what you want. You had better get used to it. Besides, you asked for it.

你不能總是得到你想要的。你最好快點適應。再説了。這是你自己造成的。

Kelvin: Sorry, I was being a pest.

對不起。我那時很討人厭。

I do not believe this is really happening! I know I should give you my blessing, because you have made a good start. This is just harder than I thought. I am still trying to live with it.

我不敢相信這件事情真的成真了！我知道我應該給你我的祝福。你已經有了一個好的開始。這只是比我想像中的難。我還在試著接受。

Vivienne: Can we just drop it? The past is the past. You have got to let it go. I am happy now. I want you to be that too.

我們可以別談這個了嗎？過去的已經過去了。你必須忘了這件事。現在很快樂。我也想要你快樂。

Kelvin: Yeah. There are plenty of fish in the sea, right?

嗯。天涯何處無芳草。對嗎？

Adrian: Yes. We are going to go now. Nice to meet you Kelvin.

沒錯。我們要走了。很高興認識你。Kelvin。

Part 5

 辦公室心情隨筆

 Kelvin:

What was Vivienne doing with that client? She looked at that client like that, It's like she was sending some kind of message. I hate it when she is doing that. I am not going to pretend that I did not see that. I have to tell her that I am not okay with it. Okay, she is just not going to admit it. Is she saying that this is my fault? It is totally her problem, not mine. How am I not mature? I am acting just normal. This is crazy, is she going to break up with me just because of this? Is she ashamed of being angry or what? Okay, then, I cannot stand this anymore. I've never expected this relationship to last long anyway. It is right to end this relationship.

Vivienne 跟那個客戶剛剛是在幹嘛？她那樣看那個客戶，就好像她在傳達什麼訊息一樣。當她那樣做的時候我很討厭。我不會假裝我沒有看到。我要告訴她我有多不能接受。好，她就是不會承認。她現在再說這是我的錯嗎？這完全是她的問題，不是我。我怎麼不成熟了？我表現的很正常。這真是瘋了。她要因為這個跟我分手嗎？她是惱羞成怒嗎還是什麼？好吧，我也不能再忍受了。我從不期待這段關係會持久。結束這段關係是對的。

Is that Vivienne there? She looks good. Who is that guy next to her? That quick? Okay, I will go say hi and find out. It is really her new guy. This is quite embarrassing. Now I just realized that I am still in love with her. I will probably just going to say all these for the last time. Okay, looks like there is no turning back.

在那裡的是 Vivienne 嗎？她看起來很好。那個在她旁邊的男的是誰啊？這麼快？好。我要去跟她打招呼然後得到答案。這真的是她新男友。這還蠻尷尬的。現在我才意識到我還愛著她。我可能要最後一次說這些話了。好吧,看起來回不了頭了。

 Vivienne:

What? I was just doing my job and I was just talking to a client normally. There was nothing between me and that client. How come he always thinks that much? I have to let him know that I can't stand this anymore. We aren't even communicating. We just do not share the same values. I cannot concentrate on my work and be professional if every time he is acting like this. I really want to end this now. Now he agrees to it.

什麼?我只是在做我的工作,而且我跟那個客戶是很正常的講話。我跟那個客戶之間又沒什麼。為什麼他總是想那麼多?我必須讓他知道我不能再忍受這個了。我們根本雞同鴨講。我們就是觀念不同。如果他每次都要這樣,我無法專注於我的工作和專業。我真的想結束這一切了。現在他同意了。

Oh, it's Kelvin. I should introduce him to my new boyfriend. This is not awkward to me. What is he doing now? Now he is making this awkward. My new boyfriend is here why would he say all these in front of him? He is still the same. He really needs to grow up. Can he just shut up? He is making me feel mad now. I have to make him stop now. I do not want to pick a fight with Adrian later. I have to let Kelvin know that I am better off without him. I want him to be happy, too. Yes, now he gets it. Yes, we should go.

噢,是 Kelvin。我應該介紹他給我的新男朋友。這對我來說不尷尬。他現在在做什麼?現在他讓這變尷尬了。我的新男友在這裡,他在他面前講這些做什麼?他還是一樣。他真的需要長大。他可以閉嘴嗎?

Part 5

他現在讓我覺得生意。 我必須讓他停止。我不想等下跟 Adrian 吵架。
我要讓 Kelvin 知道，沒有他我更好。我也想要他快樂。好，現在他懂
了。對，我們該走了。

好好用句型

★ **Who is to blame for this?**
這件事該怪誰？

> Or you can say:
>
> - Who is to accuse for this?
>   這件事該責怪誰？
> - Who is to get at for this?
>   這件事該怪誰？

★ **There you go again!**
你又來了

> Or you can say:
>
> - You are doing it again!
>   你又再做同樣的事了。（以負面性質為多）
> - You are at it again!
>   你又揪著同樣的事不放了。

★ **Will you please stop being childish?**
可以拜託別再小孩子氣了**?**
Don't be childish.
不要孩子氣了；別無理取鬧

> Or you can say:
>
> - Don't be such a child.
>   不要像小孩子一樣

- Stop fussing!
  不要無理取鬧

心理小測試

愛情心理

Q 在某天上班途中。你看到一間畫廊裡面展示著一幅美麗的水彩小鳥圖畫。這幅畫勾起了你某種回憶或想法。那是什麼？

A：你曾有過一個另一半喜歡小鳥。這讓你想起了你們曾經的點滴。

B：小時候，你曾不小心讓飼養的小鳥飛走了，你想起了當時的悔恨。

C：院子裡常飛來小鳥，而你會餵食。你好奇那隻小鳥現在在哪裡？

D：小鳥真自由。如果自己能像小鳥一樣自由飛翔，該有多好！

測驗結果
請見下頁

辦公室篇

貿易篇

業務篇

行銷篇

感情篇

測驗結果

A：你是一個浪漫的人，你時常戀舊，你容易沉浸在回憶裡，你有自我陶醉的傾向，在戀愛中，你擅長編織像童話一般的謊言，以博取他人的同情，然後甩掉包袱後能夠繼續逍遙在自己的世界裡。

B：你內心深處有不安全感，這暗喻著與戀人分手的預期心理。在生活中你卻會將不安隱藏起來，你與異性交往時，一臉無辜的笑容是你的招牌。

C：你有著「隨意支配對方的心理」。你應該非常自信，認為自己總是正確的。戀情中也通常主動。你通常會說出「我這是為你好」的話，一副為對方好的樣子，而實際上不過是將行為正當化而編出的藉口。

D：嚮往自由的心態，是你目前寫照。你嚮往一種自由無慮的生活，但是目前的境況可能是限制你自由的。你正處在一種穩定，但是缺乏新鮮感的戀情中，你認為這段感情羈絆了你的自由。

心理知識補一補

 依附理論

　　精神分析學家約翰鮑比在 1950 年代時提出了「依附理論」（**Attachment Theory**），指的是一個（或一組）關於為了得到安全感而尋求親近另一人的心理傾向的理論。當這一個被依附的人在場時，會感到安心，不在場時則會感到焦慮。

　　這個理論通常被廣泛地應用在兒童發展心理學當中，研究對象以嬰兒及幼兒為主。研究發現，隨著孩童的年紀漸長，對於母親（或是養育者）的依附行為會有所不同，而依附的程度也會漸漸變弱。依附行為則可分成兩大類：1. 安全依附型；2. 焦慮依附型。依附行為的不同則與嬰兒的生長環境，以及養育者的背景有相當性的關連。而心理學家也指出在成長時所經歷到的依附關係，會影響到長大後的戀愛態度，在戀愛時則會重現與兒時相同的依附行為類型。

　　在一些研究當中有提到屬於焦慮依附型裡一種的「抵抗型依附」的男性容易有外遇的行為，而也比較容易在外遇關係中給對方承諾。

辦公室篇

貿易篇

業務篇

行銷篇

感情篇

Leader 020

職場英語占「心」術
成為人見人愛的職場大贏家

作　　　者	何宜璞
封面構成	高鍾琪
內頁構成	菩薩蠻數位文化有限公司

發 行 人	周瑞德
企劃編輯	丁筠馨
執行編輯	陳欣慧
校　　　對	陳韋佑、饒美君
印　　　製	大亞彩色印刷製版股份有限公司
初　　　版	2015 年 6 月
定　　　價	新台幣 349 元
出　　　版	力得文化
電　　　話	(02) 2351-2007
傳　　　真	(02) 2351-0887
地　　　址	100 台北市中正區福州街 1 號 10 樓之 2
E - m a i l	best.books.service@gmail.com

港澳地區總經銷	泛華發行代理有限公司
地　　　　　址	香港新界將軍澳工業邨駿昌街 7 號 2 樓
電　　　　　話	(852) 2798-2323
傳　　　　　真	(852) 2796-5471

國家圖書館出版品預行編目(CIP)資料

職場英語占「心」術，成為人見人愛的職場
大贏家/ 何宜璞著. -- 初版. -- 臺北
市：力得文化, 2015.06
　　面；　公分. -- (Leader ; 20)
ISBN 978-986-91914-0-1(平裝)

1.英語 2.職場 3.會話 4.心理測驗

805.188　　　　　　　　　　　　104009260